I0544012

Bloodbane

A Maro Prakk Novella: Book 2

Copyright

Edited by: Jonathan Oliver
https://reedsy.com/#/freelancers/jon-o

Book Cover by: Ivan Zanchetta © 2025
https://www.bookcoversart.com

Map by: Hannah Marie
Instagram: hannah_marie._artwork
https://hannahmarieartwork.blog

Author's Socials:
https://www.outpostdire.com
https://www.patreon.com/OutpostDire
X: @OutpostDire
Instagram: @Outpost_Dire

Works By The Author

The Dark Legacy Series: (Grimdark Fantasy)
The Bearer of Secrets
Mark of the Profane
The Jackal of Shades

The Maro Prakk Novella Series: (Western Fantasy)
Red Creek
Bloodbane

The Warmaster Series: (Military Sci-fi Fantasy)
The Demon's Fate
Decimation Protocol (2026)

Other Works:
Flawed to the Core: Building Memorable Characters and Writing
The Dark Portal (Sci-fi Thriller)
For Heathens of Heaven (poetry)

Dedication

Many years ago, I entered a writing contest, presenting the first two chapters of the original book Maro appears in. In Maro's chapter, I had a throwaway line—at the time—and one of the judges commented, "I'd love to read that story." All these years later, it still rattled around in my head. Well, this isn't that story, but it's the start of it. So, here's to that judge who planted the seeds.

Acknowledgements

To my editor, Jon Oliver.
To the members of House Eti.
To alpha and beta readers far and wide.
Many thanks for keeping me on the path and coming back for more.

Map

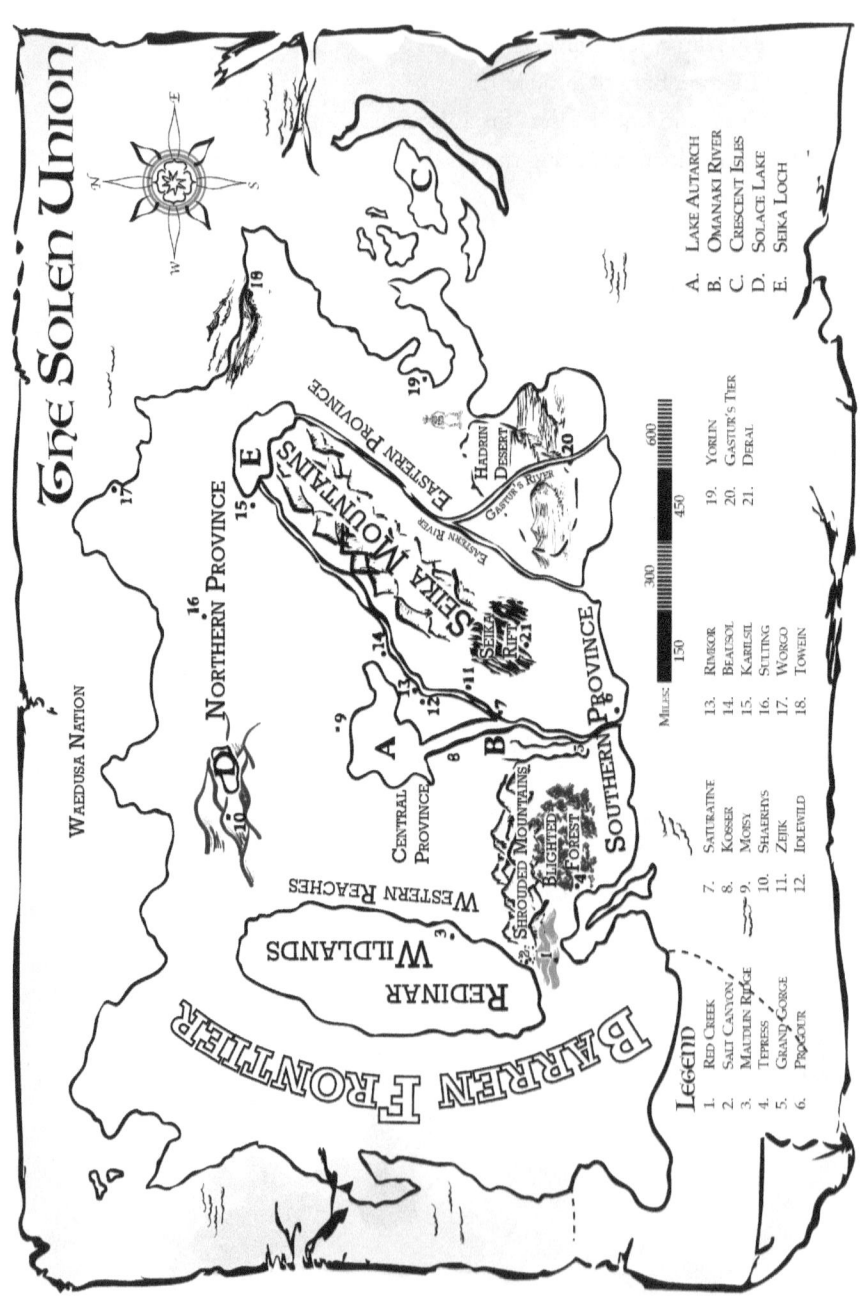

The Solen Union

Waedusa Nation

Northern Province

Central Province

Western Reaches

Rednar Wildlands

Barren Frontier

Southern Province

Seika Mountains

Seika Rift

Eastern Province

Hadrin Desert

Gastor's River

Eastern River

Legend

1. Red Creek
2. Salt Canyon
3. Mautlin Ridge
4. Tepress
5. Grand Gorge
6. Progur

7. Saturatine
8. Kosser
9. Mosey
10. Shaerhys
11. Zerik
12. Idlewild

13. Rimkor
14. Beatsol
15. Karlisd
16. Sulting
17. Worco
18. Towen

19. Yorlin
20. Gastur's Tier
21. Deral

22. Shrouded Mountains
23. Blighted Forest

Miles 150   300   450   600

A. Lake Altarch
B. Omanaki River
C. Crescent Isles
D. Solace Lake
E. Seika Loch

Epigraph

Beauty is the veneer obscuring the soul.

Chapter 1: Gold And Garnet

Suspect that your friend may be your enemy, and treat your enemy as your friend; one day their roles may reverse—The Book of Chaos, The Sacral Compendium

Only a few times in life stick with a man long after the deed has passed: the first time he laid with a woman, the first time he took a life, and the first time he feels a pistol pressed into the back of his head.

Maro was experiencing the latter at the moment.

"Do nothing stupid," said the man holding the pistol. His thick accent made understanding him difficult.

"Stranger," Maro replied, "the only thing I'm thinking about right now's not shitting myself."

"Good; you not stupid."

Well, that's fucking debatable.

"Nice and easy," said Pistol Man.

Damn the Autarch, what in the seven hells is he saying?

It sounded as if the man's swollen tongue stuck to the roof of his mouth.

Maro let out a pent-up breath. He'd been caught at a bad time, an awkward moment, the tail-end of a fistfight with his quarry. The hog tie for his hands lay half-finished, and Maro stopped while straddling the man. Introducing a third person put the scuffle on pause. Maro glanced down at his victim, the man losing the confrontation, and he wasn't smiling. This newcomer wasn't his friend, either.

There were a lot of things Maro could've said, but such words fled him at the crucial moment, so he stuck with the simple, even if it made him sound like a backwater country bumpkin. "So, can I help you?"

"Maybe," said the foreigner with the gun. "He's my bounty, stranger."

A bounty hunter? Really?

"Funny," Maro countered. "I'd say you're interfering with the apprehension of mine."

The man circled around Maro's left side, coming into his peripheral. The cold, hard pistol never left his skull, the barrel dragged across his scalp. Between the darkness of night and the flickering firelight, not to mention glancing at him from the corner of his eye, Maro couldn't discern his features.

Not the most important thing, at the moment.

"You bounty hunter?" Pistol Man asked. "Name? I may have heard."

I fucking doubt that!

Now that the man was closer and upwind, Maro detected the not-so-subtle scent of wet dog.

How'd this bastard get the drop on me?

Maro grunted. "I'm new. Maro Prakk. Joined up in Tepress under Horace."

The other paused for a moment. "I've heard." He nodded more to himself, then waved a dismissive hand. "Nine months, yes? You have proof?"

Maro frowned, his eyes narrowing, trying to follow the man's words. This foreigner couldn't articulate his words for shit, a second or third language at best. "I'll grab my chit, so long as you don't get trigger-happy."

"Left hand, nice and easy."

Maro reached into his coat pocket, fishing for the small metal disc with his name stamped on the back. On the front, it held the initials BHG for the Bounty Hunter's Guild.

They ain't the most imaginative, but gotta keep it simple for the stupid, which is seventy-five percent of the population.

Below the initials read: *Tepress*, where Maro had signed up. Grasping it between two fingers, Maro withdrew his hand with deliberate care. Holding it aloft, Pistol Man plucked it from his fingers. His fingers were rather cold when they brushed Maro's.

"Ha, you bounty hunter!"

Damn the Autarch, he keeps dropping words, makes him sound ignorant.

The pistol withdrew from Maro's head, and the wet-dog foreigner holstered it. Maro let out a held breath.

"Runnel Bloodbane." The man thumped his chest with pride. "Bounty hunter!"

The tension leached out of Maro's shoulders, and he finished hog-tying the prisoner's hands, who squirmed and grunted but otherwise lost the will to fight. Now, with the two of them, escape turned impossible. Checking the taut rope, Maro dismounted the criminal and stood to his full height. No longer preoccupied, he sized up Runnel Bloodbane.

The man stood taller than most, but Maro held the lead by half a boot. In fact, Maro once heard his height put him in the top five percent of men across the world of Atar.

Fat lot of good that does me, not when attached to this face.

Runnel, however, resembled an animal, the kind you find in a dark, cramped cave—one who'd been starving all winter and ready to eat. Not to mention covered in fur too thick for a bullet to pierce. A bushy, black beard obscured most his face and hung in tangled strains down to his torso. The same curly mess roosted on his head, and both together resembled a helmet and face protection rather than actual hair, and if Maro had to guess, attributed to half his smell.

Probably keeps him warm, too. I hate him already.

Runnel went well with the surrounding terrain, rolling hills with tall, wild grass, and a smattering of trees as varied as the cock pox in a brothel. Maro heard rumors of caves in the hills further south, and Bloodbane might've stumbled out of one.

"Hey, fellas," the man on the ground said, his voice shaky but coated with a country twang. "Not sure what's going on here, but you're mistaken."

Runnel sent a swift kick into the man's gut, and the wind rushed out of him in a sudden gust.

"Quiet," Runnel barked in his maddening accent, but his voice brokered no argument. Maro used similar tones while in the army.

"What'd you do that for?" whined the man. "I didn't mean nothing."

Runnel pulled out his pistol and cocked the hammer back.

"Hey!" Maro said, but Runnel was already kneeling beside the man.

"Open," Bloodbane said, shoving the metal barrel into the man's mouth.

Maro contemplated interceding, but the wanted poster said dead or alive. Plus, the interaction would give him a moment to evaluate the foreign bounty hunter.

"We talk, just hunters, and you lay quiet. Be like good whore, no talk with dick in mouth. If quiet, I won't shoot. Deal?"

The wanted man nodded frantically.

Runnel dipped his head once and stood, holstering his weapon. He stretched his arms out wide, standing on his toes. "By Autarch, I love hunting."

Maro, with a slow movement to not draw attention, turned his body sideways so the man couldn't see his holster or drawing hand. Runnel wore a massive coat, and while not fur, it looked like the dark brown of a bear.

Damn thing's half my weight.

"Hmm. Well then, you won't mind showing me yours, would you?" Maro knew he risked offending the man, but better than going on blind faith. If Runnel Bloodbane was one of them, he'd have a chit and adhere to the code.

Runnel's dark emerald eyes narrowed and hardened; they looked like flint chips, or the sharp end of steel.

Shit, a shootout?

Maro only had one ball in his single-shot pistol, but so did Runnel.

The whites of Runnel's teeth split the dark, tangled growth on his face. "Smart kid! Sure."

His hot breath almost made the ex-soldier vomit in his mouth. Putrid would curl cream; this shit would decompose live bodies.

Bloodbane fished for his chit while Maro took a step back from the reeking plume and mulled over being called a kid. A few months ago, Maro celebrated his first birthday out of the army, and he, a ripe old twenty-four, with all the shit he'd seen and done, had abandoned childhood long ago.

"Ah," Runnel said, finding it and pulling it out, "here." He flipped it to Maro, and his attention reverted to the tied-up man.

Maro didn't miss the gaze, and he took a moment to size up the newest member of their trio. Runnel resembled an ox … that got fucked by a grizzly bear, and he outweighed Maro by a few mountains. Thick of chest, arms, and legs, not to mention the slight keg around the gut, Maro wouldn't stand a chance. From the collar of his gray shirt, Maro spied a thick forest sprouting from his chest.

This foreigner would snap me like a twig.

Maro was tall, gangly, and filled with brittle bones; the army folk took to calling him Scarecrow, and the name stuck. He flipped the chit over in his hands, and on the back, Runnel Bloodbane's name. On the front, under the initials BHG, he found Goldar stamped in the metal.

"What parts are you from?" Maro asked.

"Sindel," Runnel answered without delay. He turned his attention to Maro.

"Heard of it, but where is it?"

"North. Different country. Waedusa."

Maro grunted.

Explains the accent.

"What?"

Maro shrugged. "Nothing. Never knew anyone coming out of that ass crack of a place."

For a moment, Runnel's face went placid, still, stony with anger, and his eyes darkened like a thunderhead on the distant horizon. Then, he tilted his head and gave a belly-rumbling laugh.

"Huh huh huh. Ass crack! You right!" He wiped a tear away from the corner of his eye. "But come," Runnel said, slapping him on the arm. The impact almost made Maro stagger a step.

Damn, that's going to bruise.

Bloodbane waved his arms as he spoke. "We sit, we eat," he pointed down at the man tied up, "we talk about friend." Runnel moved closer to the crackling fire and took a seat, leaning against Maro's saddle on the ground.

I was going to sit there …

Runnel pulled a bag from the other side of his body, and for a moment, Maro thought he'd brought his own. Instead, the man produced Maro's pack, and he rummaged through the contents, pulling out his stale bread, hardened cheese, and jerky.

What the—?

"Not much here," Runnel grumbled with disapproval. "I get bag." He hefted himself up and disappeared into the darkness.

Well, it ain't like I offered to share.

The crickets, as if being granted permission to chirp again, struck up a tune, filling the silence. Maro reclaimed his seat in front of the saddle, keeping his eyes on the man he'd hog-tied. Maro's saddle, a thing of beauty and comfort, was his most prized possession other than his horse, Bastard. In the nine months of hunting, Maro had spent every crown he earned, which wasn't much. The nice pile of coins he'd received for all the sold weapons after rescuing the girl, Maribel, fled faster than a wife leaving a man who lost all his money. But after paying his dues, buying a new saddle, finding a livable hovel, purchasing a cantankerous young mare, adding to his sparse collection of tattered clothes, he didn't have two coins to rub together, and the most entertaining and affordable thing involved his hand and some alone time.

Sad story of my life.

Runnel returned, his bag hanging from his right hand. When he reached Maro, he leaned down, plucked the saddle up from behind Maro, and dumped it on the ground before reclaiming his seat.

What a son of a bitch!

Bloodbane leaned back against his reacquired backrest and opened the top of his pack. "Nice saddle. I buy!"

Maro grunted. "Ain't for sale."

"Everything's for sale, for right price!"

Not everything.

Maro thought back to one of the many reasons he left the army: his sadistic captain with nonexistent morals. Runnel pulled out a flask from his pack, took a swig, and passed it off.

Maro shook his head at the offered drink, but damn, did his mouth water. He could almost smell the sweet succor from here.

"No?" Runnel asked, surprised.

"Don't partake anymore."

Bloodbane gave a single shake of the head. "Don't trust someone who doesn't drink." He leaned close, and Maro breathed in the spirit fumes. By the gods, he wanted a drink now. "Hard for us to work together."

"Hmm. You won't like me when I'm drunk."

"Oh?" Runnel leaned close again with mocking tones. "Stick Man be angry drunk?"

"Something like that."

Runnel took another swig, screwed the lid on, and dropped it into his pack. He sniffed through his nose, then rubbed it until it turned red in the firelight. He pointed to the man tied up. "You know?"

Maro's eyes went to the prisoner. "Yeah, he's my prisoner, after all. Tristan Bolag. Wanted for stagecoach robbery and horse thieving."

Bloodbane grinned ear to ear and nodded his head in affirmation. "No."

"What?"

"Not him. I mean, yes, it's … er, alias. He has other name, and I want words."

Maro took a moment to collect his thoughts. "What kind of words?" The fire crackled with a pop, punctuating the question. "The kind that kill?"

"Important ones." Runnel cocked an eyebrow at him. "Make me rich." He tapped his finger to his nose. "Be smart, let me have."

Maro's eyes flickered to the man's fingers, not the one tapping his nose, but the others. There, a gold and garnet ring clung to his middle finger with an engraving on the side, but Maro couldn't make out the details.

"So, I go talk?"

Maro swallowed. He knew firsthand the methods of getting someone to talk, and he didn't want to venture down that path anytime soon.

Or ever.

"Who do you think he is?"

Bloodbane chuckled, his face turning a deep shade of cherry, probably from the alcohol. "You love this." He spread his hands out in a sweeping gesture. "'Chester 'Jester' Pen—Pen—Pen; eh, what is word?" He growled in frustration, and from inside his coat, produced a folded wanted poster. He unfolded it and showed it to Maro.

"Pennyworth."

Bloodbane nodded, satisfied, folding it back up and stuffing it into his tunic. "Pennyworth." Maro didn't react, and Bloodbane's brow frowned at him. "You don't know name?"

"No."

Runnel gave a single nod. "Every guild I go, I take poster. No man hunts mine."

"Didn't realize we called dibs."

Bloodbane chuckled again and punched Maro in the arm. "You funny! Why you look like someone kicked dog?"

Damn it, another bruise.

Maro drew his lower lip between his teeth; unsure of what to say, other than he didn't have a dog, he chose not to respond. His stomach growled, a reminder that his newest guest said he had food to share.

"Him," Bloodbane said, pointing his finger, "shot woman in card game. She showed ..."

Bloodbane pantomimed a woman's generous bosom.

"Who shoots woman in chest? Ruined good breasts, no? If woman shows me," he chuckled again, a grin splitting the dark, unruly facial growth, "I show her something, too. Eh? Eh?"

Runnel elbowed him in the arm a few times, and though he wouldn't complain, that shit hurt, especially when you're all skin and bones.

Another damn bruise. Man's too rough.

Maro glanced up at the night sky.

By the Autarch, why did you make people like this?

He lowered his gaze and looked at the prisoner. "That true? You shot a woman in the tits?"

Tristan Bolag shook his head, fear lighting his face, and his twangy voice peeled the night.

"Look, mister, I don't know this man, or anything he said I done. I was just mindin' my business when you assaulted me this evenin'."

He held up his hands.

"If ya cut me loose, I'll go on my merry. I won't seek no retribution or nothin'."

"Liar!" Bloodbane said with a wave of his hand. "All Cosams lie!"

Maro grunted and swung his head to Bloodbane.

Well, that's a gut punch.

"Say what now?" Maro asked.

Bloodbane gave him a double take. "Not you, him, lout. You okay Cosam."

"And what does that make you?"

"Sional, no?"

Maro cracked a smile and rolled his eyes. When he turned his head away, he frowned.

Great, a jackass with jokes.

Sional were dark complected, and Bloodbane was the antithesis.

"Mium," Runnel announced.

That caused Maro's head to whip back around. His neck cracked.

"No shit?"

He rubbed at the base of his neck.

Miums were the palest Atarians, living in near-frigid conditions year-round. They didn't have summer, and Maro doubted the vast majority had ever seen the ocean, let alone a nice beach and tropical weather. The man traveled far from his home, which was … astounding, to say the least. Then again, if anyone other than the Cosam ethnicity was in this land, they traversed far from their place of birth.

Runnel held up his pale hands. "Goat milk."

Maro shrugged. "Never seen one of you. How'd you come from … where did you say you were from again?"

"Sindel," Bloodbane said with his thick accent. It rolled off his fat tongue. He held up a finger, shaking it at him. "As you know. But … " He waved to Tristan or Jester Chester, or whoever the hell he was, "… I want words, and have now."

"Look, mister, I done told ya," Tristan Bolag stammered, "I ain't the guy. I've never even—"

"No lie," Bloodbane snapped, "or I cut tongue. So says Sacral book. Will make taking information harder. You write?"

Tristan stuttered. "A little, only a few words."

Bloodbane gestured as if the problem was solved. "I won't break hands."

"Hold on," Maro said. "Not to call you a liar or say you're mistaken, but I only got your word he's this Chester fellow. You got proof, Bloodbane?"

Runnel stared at him for a few moments, his face flexing between hard and soft. "Poster."

"Let me see it."

Runnel reached into his tunic and retrieved a folded, yellowed parchment. Maro hoped he didn't have to listen to him read it. Instead, the Mium handed it over, and Maro sighed in relief.

Maro read aloud. "'Wanted: Dead. Chester 'Jester' Pennyworth. Wanted for crimes of theft and robbery in Tepress, cheating at an establishment of fine order in Moisy, shooting a woman in the breasts in Moisy, illegal dueling and murder in Grand Gorge, assault of a prostitute in Deral, arson in Red Creek, and …'" Maro dropped the parchment. "The list goes on."

The mention of Red Creek hit Maro harder than he thought, stealing his breath. He'd thought about the girl, Maribel, a handful of times since joining the guild, and he wondered how she fared. Had he made the right call to give her to The House of Lust and Candor?

Maro, you ain't no dad. You can't take care of yourself, let alone a child. You did right.

If he did, why didn't he feel great about it? It didn't make the doubt any less encumbering.

Bloodbane pointed to the poster. "What his looks?"

Maro began reading again. "Fair complected, blond hair, and blue of eye. Clean shaven, standing of average height and build, often seen wearing two pistols on the hip."

"There!" Tristan said, latching on to the words as a lifeline thrown to him in rushing water. "I ain't got two pistols! Ya can check my things!"

"Hmm. The description sounds like my wanted poster."

"Ah, yes!" Bloodbane said, holding up a finger. "Yours say tattoo?"

Maro eyed Runnel. "No, no mention of a tattoo."

Bloodbane gave him a wolfish smile and pointed for Maro to continue reading.

"Identifying marks: tattoo of two playing cards on left ass cheek, an Ace and a Jester."

"Wha—?" Tristan stammered. "That's—that's just silly, fellas."

Maro gazed at the criminal. The man's eyes were wide, and that might be fear or shock. The sheen of sweat on his head could be from their tussle, but Maro sensed something more. He stood.

"One way to find out."

Maro handed the parchment back to the other hunter and stepped over to Tristan, who still lay on the ground.

"Alright, let's get this done. Drop your pants."

"What? I ain't going to do no such thing! That's indecent! Y'all are a bunch of perverts!"

Maro sighed through his nose.

"I ain't gonna poke you, just see if you have the tattoo or not. If you don't, you're in the clear."

"It's inhumane!"

"I help," Bloodbane said from behind, and he got to his feet.

When he stood beside Maro, he moved faster than expected, snatching Tristan by the clothes and rolling him over to his stomach. He put his foot on the man's hand and leaned over it. Tristan cried out. Bloodbane bent and set his knife against the criminal's arm.

"Move and you get cut. Maro, go."

Well, that'll make it easier.

Maro pulled his own blade, reached down, cut Tristan's belt, and jerked the pants down. A jester stared back up at him.

"*Booci*," Bloodbane said in his native tongue.

Maro peered over at him.

That word sounds too much like the sweetest thing known to man.

The stench wafting up was terrible, and Maro straightened as quick as he dared. "I'll be damned. Who gets a tattoo on their ass?"

"Chester Jester," Bloodbane said, standing, lifting his foot from the man's hand, and the knife from his arm.

"Hmm. I mean, what drives a man to have someone stab him in the ass with needles?" Apparently, where Runnel hailed from, rhetorical questions existed because he didn't answer. "Alright, so where does that leave us?"

Bloodbane smiled with a vigorous nod. "I have chat, you turn in."

Chester squirmed on the ground, trying to recover some of his dignity by pulling up his pants with his hands bound.

Maro didn't believe Runnel for a moment.

The man might try to kill me once he's done.

"Just like that?"

The other pulled on his curly, shaggy beard and gave a single dip of his head.

"What does he have that's so important?"

"Information."

"About?"

"An … eh, animal, monsters."

Maro's eyes widened, not in fear, but eagerness.

"What kind of monster?"

"Much money to kill. Money and deeds bring fame, which bring women, and more kills, and more money and fame, and more women. Good cycle, no?"

"Hmm."

"What? You think I cheat? You have body."

"Body?" Chester said from the ground. "Now, wait a second, fellas."

"Quiet, or I cut tongue."

Maro grew pensive. This wouldn't end well. Runnel might turn on him in an instant. Chester could lie until he turned blue, and Runnel wouldn't know until much later, little incentive to be honest when your life hung in the balance. True, Bloodbane could beat the prisoner until his knuckles were bloody, and he'd be no closer to the truth.

"He ain't going to talk," Maro said.

"I make."

"No, he ain't got the incentive to." Maro faced Bloodbane. "He'll lie his ass off to save his hide. You won't know until you go there to find out, but if you give him his life, he might tell the truth."

"Might."

"Might's better than nothing. If he lies and dies, you've got nothing."

Runnel cocked an eyebrow as his hand swept through the tangled mess on his face. "And you? No money if cut loose."

Maro nodded. "If you bring me in on this deal you're about to make, I won't come away empty-handed."

Runnel stopped stroking his beard and shook his head. "No, my money. I have lifestyle."

Maro's eyes widened, then drew together as he scrutinized the man. Judging by his appearance and the stench, he reeked of the wilderness. "What lifestyle?"

"Women; very expensive." Runnel shrugged. "Soap for beard."

Maro grunted. "That puts us back at the start, him dead and you without certainty whether he told the truth. Cut me in on the deal for twenty-five percent."

Bloodbane's emerald eyes hardened, but they softened as he thought. "You hunted beasts?"

Maro shook his head.

"Not worth twenty-five percent."

"I learn fast. Besides, it's the other part of our gig, hunting and killing beasts. I need to learn."

"Partnership?"

"Yeah."

"Fifteen percent."

"I've got to eat. Twenty."

"You green ears, use for distraction. I kill beast as he eats you."

Green ears? What the fuck's that? I bet he meant wet behind the ears. Well, he's got a point there, sorta.

"You ain't got nothing to worry about if you rake in one hundred percent of the profit, besides, I've got five years in the army."

Bloodbane waved another dismissive hand and nodded. "Army not count. But you survive, I only get eighty."

13

Maro sighed through his nose. "I doubt you're going after small game. You'll need help, and you'll have to hire other bounty hunters, and they won't work for so little. It's the best deal out there. I get to learn, take a little profit, and you reap all the fame and women you want."

Runnel nodded, but Maro sensed his reluctance, but maybe mentioning the cost of other hunters would make him reconsider.

"Okay." Bloodbane held out his hand and shook Maro's. Runnel crushed his hand and pulled him close. "You fuck me, and I make you little girl, yes?"

Maro leaned back as the man released his grip.

Don't know what he means, and I don't care to find out.

"Sure."

Maro ambled closer to Chester.

"Alright, shit sack, you've heard everything, so that's the deal. Start talking."

"No!" Chester said. "You'll hunt me once I leave out of here."

"You'd deserve," Bloodbane chimed in.

Maro shook his head. "No, I won't hunt you, at least not for a while, unless you lie."

"How long's a while?"

Maro shrugged.

"A year, or I don't say nothing!"

Maro gave a single chuckle. "Six months, and not a day later. If you leave the territory and stay underground, who knows how long you can last? May come a time when people forget all about you."

"And the other bounty hunters?"

Maro shrugged again. "Can't make promises for others. This is the best you're gonna get. Talk and live, or don't talk, and I'll let Bloodbane soften you up. Choice is yours."

He needed little persuasion. Runnel spoke in low tones for over an hour, and it seemed the grizzly man kept up his intensity as they retraced details. Maro didn't care if Bloodbane wanted to keep things secretive. If Runnel double-crossed him and cut him out, he'd file a complaint with the guild master. In the short term, Maro would feel the pain of missing funds, but once word got out about Bloodbane's double-crossing ...

Runnel nodded and finally stood. "Go, leave." He cut the man free. For a moment, Chester stared at them in disbelief, then scrambled away, holding up his britches as he hobbled away in haste.

Damn, there goes two runes of work. Two hundred crowns is a lot to gamble on. Can put a dent in my rent and other needs.

A movement drew his attention, and before he could react, Bloodbane pulled his pistol, aimed at the retreating figure, and fired. Chester went down in a heap. The night life went quiet, even the wind stilled, a paused breath as if the shot was the roar of a large predator. Then, the hum of crickets, owls, and small animals scurrying about returned.

"What'd you do that for?" Maro yelled.

Bloodbane shrugged. "He shot woman's tits. Ruined good breasts."

"I gave him my word!"

Bloodbane stared at him for a moment, his face unmoving. "I didn't."

"You're missing the point!"

"No," Runnel said, shaking his head and holstering his single-fire pistol. "You said *you*. I never said. Poster says dead." Bloodbane shrugged. "He's dead. You take body; you take ten percent. Deal?"

"I don't even know how much your bounty's worth! I took it on faith."

Runnel sighed and pulled out another yellowed parchment. He held it up for Maro to see.

"Two autarchs?" Maro gasped. "Two thousand crowns?"

Bloodbane chuckled. "Nice sum. Many women. Ten percent, yes?"

Maro took a moment to think it through. Ten percent was two hundred crowns, and Chester's wanted poster was also two hundred. That'd give him the initial twenty percent they agreed on. And if Drallus, the guild master, allowed him to double-dip with the Tristan poster, well, he'd be better off, anyway. Greed made the foreign man blind; either that, or he was bad at math. But for certain, his speech sucked worse than a dead hooker.

"Alright," Maro agreed.

"Good, now question. Your saddle, how much?"

Chapter 2: Cautionary Tale

Let the joining of flesh between man and woman be a joyous occasion and remove all curses. Spurn the man who should come between husband and wife, scorn the bride who withholds such sacraments from her betrothed—The Book of Lust, The Sacral Compendium.

Maro and Bloodbane rode into Tepress in the early evening the next day. The cloudless, blue-grey sky lent aid to the chilly, early spring air. Tristan's body, wrapped in a canvas, slumped over his horse while Maro tied its lead to the horn of his saddle. Runnel resembled a bear riding astride his splotchy brown horse, and his face hadn't moved one iota since the night before, as if chiseled from irritated granite. Maro reckoned the big fella was in a bad mood since he refused to sell his saddle, but if the burly man didn't want to trade words, silence was a companion who couldn't disappoint.

Silence is gold in your pocket, and better than trying to decipher his speech.

They rode in from the southeast, the direction Maro once took to run away from Tepress and the duty of escorting a little girl home. When he set out to chase down Maribel, it'd been from the northwest side. To the south, the vegetation grew in abundance—massive oak trees, sprawling wild grass, and unforgiving rock—and much closer to the town's outskirts than on the northern side. Plus, to the north, on the way to Red Creek and the Barren Frontier, flora came sparse. Maro once slept under a few shrubs in the ass-end of nowhere, only to be roused by the hot breath of a warg.

Maro's horse, Bastard, went to the guildhall, knowing the way without any prodding. It'd become their habit over the last nine months. While he planned to retire the old boy and let him live out his days in comfort, training his mare wasn't going well, and she proved to be a stubborn bitch. So, time and again, he and Bastard hit the trail. Most trips were short jaunts to the next town over, or a day or two out in the woods, but ever since the Lanton gang, they hadn't pushed as hard.

Thank the Autarch, too. That shit was brutal.

Bastard stopped in front of the hitching post, dust coughing up from the parched earth below his hooves. It hadn't rained in a month, the winter dry and cold, and the weather hadn't turned into the scorching inferno his brittle bones yearned for. He swung out of the saddle, his long, gray trench coat swaying as he did. Bending over, he rubbed his inner thighs.

The people of Tepress were still milling about at dusk, in transit to their homes or saloons. The flowing dresses of hurrying women swayed as men scuffed their boots across wood planks near the storefronts.

A creaking wagon pulled by four horses rolled through the middle of the manure-littered, hard-packed street, heading southeast, the road they entered from. In the back, under the white, rounded canvas, he saw two children with gloomy, dirty faces, the interior packed with all their meager possessions.

Maro watched them for a time, wondering where they were headed, and what prospects awaited them at their new destination.

Law of the Land. One place's salvation is another man's damnation.

He shook his head and turned his attention back to his traveling companion. When they made eye contact, he saw Bloodbane, still in his saddle, staring at him.

"I go saloon. Must have woman."

Odd statement, considering we just arrived. Surely, he's going to wash before swapping body sweat?

The thought made him want to vomit. Maro could think of a dozen things more important than wetting his wick. Since they'd been together, Bloodbane had been about himself, but money and women took center stage for the Mium.

Hell, I ain't the easiest person to open up either.

But what words did pass between them, and Runnel's actions, told him enough.

The man's demerit's lust. He's all about money and fame. That's why he wanted my saddle.

It was why Bloodbane sought a woman now.

Everyone had a demerit, a monumental flaw to them, just like everyone belonged to a House of the Gods. Not all demerits were negative traits, but how they were incorporated could be. Maro's demerit of intolerance made him a miserable son of a bitch all the time. He couldn't stand the shortcomings of others, and no excuse proved decent enough or valid. A demerit of lawfulness would cause someone to turn in their own jaywalking mother for a pat on the head and a warm fuzzy in their chest. The slightest provocation construed as unlawful would rip someone apart on the inside until they righted the wrong.

Thank the gods I don't have that issue. Rescuing Maribel would've been a nightmare.

A demerit of lust had to be one of the craziest, but it could be worse. A demerit of obedience—or even disobedience—would make life far more insufferable. Zealotry, greed, malice, compassion, love … for these qualities to be at the forefront, forsaking all others to the detriment of all …

Horrible way to live.

"Alright," Maro grumbled.

"Come when finished. You meet someone."

Maro didn't really want to get tangled with a sweaty, worn-out floozy, and preparing himself for the worst, he said, "I ain't keen to stand in line behind you."

Bloodbane tilted his head back and laughed. "You funny man." He shook his head. "No, better. A man."

Maro cocked an eyebrow.

"I see him often," Bloodbane continued.

Maro crossed his arms. "Well, that doesn't sound any better. What you do in privacy's none of my concern, and if that's the tumble in the hay you like, I say graze away, but don't think I'll entertain such notions."

Bloodbane laughed again, his belly-rumbling—'huh huh huh'—startling a woman walking on the other side of the road. Runnel pointed. "By Autarch, Maro, you funny. No sex, talk. He makes weapons. Must know."

Thank the fucking Autarch.

"Right."

Runnel turned his horse and hurried down the road.

About to think up an excuse to not go on the hunt.

Moving closer to the second horse, Maro untied Tristan from the saddle and hefted him up on his shoulder. For a moment, he thought his knees might buckle under the weight.

One more confirmation: I'd lose a scuffle with Bloodbane.

Holding his breath and praying to the Autarch he made it, Maro hurried up the rickety, weathered steps, opened the faded door, and shuffled into the hall. Horace glanced up as he neared the counter.

"Ah, Mr. Prakk," Horace greeted, his face brightened by Maro's arrival.

Maro dropped the dead body on the floor. The corpse's head hit with a sickening crack, and Maro's stomach turned queasy. The guild hall manager leaned over the counter and peered down at the canvas-wrapped body. Horace signed Maro up nine months ago and in the dead of night; Horace thought he'd come to rob the place. The manager had long black hair sweeping past his shoulders, and a thin moustache, almost like a ink smudge above his lip.

"Who do we have here, Maro?"

The bounty hunter pulled out a folded wanted poster and slapped it down on the unvarnished counter. He spun it around to face the guild worker. The scent of sawdust, leather, and oil permeated the air, and he took a deep inhale through his nose. He'd always like the smell of this place, a timelessness, hallowed by all the hunters who'd come before. He found it comforting.

"'Tristan Bolag,'" Horace read. "Pity you didn't bring him in alive—would've been a hundred. Dead, he's only worth fifty."

Maro grunted as he reached down and pulled back the canvas so Horace could identify him.

"Yeah," Horace muttered, "that's him, alright. Let me grab the cash box."

"Wait." He pulled out another wanted poster and presented it in the same fashion.

"Chester 'Jester' Pennyworth," Horace read in a slow voice, "'wanted dead, two-hundred crowns.'" He cocked and eyebrow and peered down at Tristan. "I only see one body."

"Good … your eyes aren't shit."

Horace huffed and waved the parchment. "You can't cash in two wanted posters with only one body."

"Sure I can, if they're the same person."

Horace's eyes narrowed. "Are you telling me that Chester 'Jester' is Tristan Bolag?"

"Yup."

"He got the tattoo?"

"Checked the smelly artwork myself."

Maro glanced down at the body. He knew what happened after death, and he wouldn't be helping to verify now.

The man shit himself. I ain't dealing with the mess.

"Show me."

Maro shook his head. "You want to see? Take a whiff of his dead ass yourself."

"Check it," a new voice called out.

Maro looked left, seeing Guild Master Drallus; he hadn't heard him enter the room. Odd, considering the peg on his right leg and the unmissable waddle. Drallus was also blind in the left eye, with a deep red scar running from his hair and clean through his jawline. Add on his corpulence and wheezing breath, and Maro couldn't guess how the man's arrival surprised him.

The step, clop, step, clop of Drallus filled the silence as he came further into the room.

"Drallus."

The ex-soldier greeted him with a dip of his head.

"Maro, my boy! Glad you're still alive."

Maro only allowed Drallus to call him boy. The old, venerable hunter deserved it, giving limb and eye in service to the hunters. His rank or position within warranted respect. The former soldier in Maro could distinguish between the man and the rank, and had Drallus been an uncouth pile of shit, well, he could respect the office without liking the man who embodied it. But the guild master hadn't been that way, and the old timer took a shine to their new, young recruit.

Maro hadn't laid eyes on the man in almost three months. Between working around the clock, taking poster after wanted poster, he hadn't run into him. Drallus came around the counter, and Maro's mouth dropped open. "What haven't you been eating? You sick?"

Drallus laughed. "Nah, been listening to the advice of a medicine man. He's part of some indigenous tribe or some such out yonder."

"Hmm."

"They don't have anyone fat in their tribe, and they eat plenty."

"What's the secret?"

"They only eat animals. Meat and fat and lard all day. Of course, it helps they have all their limbs to hunt, but I thought I'd give it a try."

"Seems to be working. How much have you dropped?"

Drallus shrugged. "Don't know, but I've gone down three sizes. I need a damn rope to keep my pants up."

"Sounds like a good problem to have." Maro toed the corpse with his boot. "So, double pay, right?"

Drallus nodded, glancing down at the dead man. "If one man is, indeed, both, then yes. Is it safe to presume you have a witness?"

He nodded. "Guy by the name of Runnel Bloodbane."

Both Horace and Drallus looked up at him, their movements sudden as if he'd threatened their lives. Maro glanced between the two. The ticking of a grandfather clock in the sitting room sounded loud in the silence.

"What?" he prodded them.

"I'd be careful with him," Horace said.

"The man's a charlatan," Drallus added. "Caution would be a start, but don't let it end there. He'll do anything for a quick coin, and any job he can take to boost his ego, he'll do it. Hell, I wouldn't be surprised if that man dabbles on the other side of the law."

Well, shit, that ain't good, even for a potential partner and just this once.

Maro grunted, digesting the words. He shrugged, then spun their words back on them. "Any witnesses?"

Drallus blew out a breath. "No, I can't say for certainty, but you shouldn't let your guard down. He's the kind of man to rifle through your nightly droppings, let them dry, and sell it back to you as jerky."

"Hmm."

"I've heard stories," Horace interjected. "He went out with a group to take on the chimera. Only he returned."

"Maybe the other guys weren't professionals?"

Horace shook his head. "No, these men had been around for years. They weren't," his eyes landed on Maro, and he gave a sheepish shrug, "green like ya."

Fair point, so long as he's referring to the bounty hunting business.

"We're talking close to ten years on the average," Horace said. "Granted, a chimera's nasty business, and they didn't have anything palladium, but someone else should've survived."

Maro blinked a few times and frowned. "What's this about palladium?"

Horace gazed at him as if he'd said the stupidest thing imaginable.

"Palladium. Ya know, the stuff our most valuable currency is made of? The autarch—a thousand crowns?"

Maro rolled his eyes. "What does money have to do with beast hunting?"

"Nothing," Drallus interrupted, "besides that it costs so damn much. Palladium's more than currency. It's the one thing that works on the majority of monsters in our world. Ever hear the tale of a silver knife killing a werewolf?"

Maro nodded.

"Palladium. So little of the precious metal is left, and that's worth more than gold or silver."

"How much more?"

"About three or four times," Horace said.

"Six, by my reckoning," Drallus corrected. "A blade infused with palladium does wonders on any beast you're trying to kill; you need it, or you won't survive. Sure, there are some other ways you can kill something: freezing it, fire, choking it, breaking its neck, but the chances are slim. Start slashing with a special knife or sword, and you've got yourself a corpse."

"Damn." He chewed his lip. "How much does something like that cost?"

"More than ya got," Horace conceded with a smile.

Drallus chuckled. "Boy, you'd have to save half of your bounties for at least half a dozen years before you'd be close."

Shit. There goes my life.

"That's why most folks team up," Drallus continued. "Not many people can afford the weapons, so they do it the old-fashioned way and wrestle it by hand, overwhelm by numbers."

Maro scratched the dark stubble on his jawline. "So, two people taking on a beast by themselves without palladium is—"

"—Suicide," Horace finished.

"Hmm."

"Why?" Drallus queried. "What have you got yourself into?"

"I'm supposed to kill something with Runnel."

Horace groaned, but Drallus spoke, "What?"

Maro shrugged.

"You don't know?"

"No."

"Well, Bloodbane doesn't have any palladium weapons."

"You're gonna die, son," Horace said, echoing the words he once imparted when they first met.

"You doubted me before."

"A gang's one thing, a monster's something else."

Drallus waved the comments away and pulled Maro by the shoulder. "Let me tell you something, my boy. Don't trust the man. He could leave you to die. He's got questionable character, and only cares about money and fame. If you go, at least ask him this: does the beast have two legs or four? If two, you might have a chance. If four, well…" He held up his hands in askance.

"Right." He paused, his eyes slipping from Drallus to Horace, who was rummaging for the cash box, and back to the guild master. "Any more headway on Avardi?"

"The banker?" Drallus asked, his brow cocked. He shook his head. "That man's been on the straight and narrow since you wiped out the Lanton gang. We notified Lawman Hugo, but other than him, only the three of us in this room know about it. Trust me, we've been keeping an eye on him. Once he gets bold enough, he'll slip up, and we'll nail him."

How? I destroyed all traces of evidence like a damn fool.

There wasn't a day that went by when Maro didn't kick himself for stupidity. If he would've let one of those shits live to bring back and stand trial, well, he would've sung like a canary in a coal mine. Then, he remembered the birds warned of death, and such a comparison was about as useful as bringing a saddle to a whore's bedroom when she asked if you wanted a ride.

Whatever.

The jangle of the cashbox behind him pulled his back to the counter.

"Two hundred and fifty crowns is my count," Horace said. Maro didn't say anything. Had the man been wrong, he would've pointed out the error. He waited as the manager counted out the coin and scooped it up once he finished.

"Ya going out with Bloodbane, aren't ya?" Horace inquired.

Maro dipped his head in acknowledgement.

"Be careful, watch your back, and think everything through three times before ya commit."

I do that anyway, but I'll make it four.

"And, remember what I told you about the legs," Drallus said as he hobbled behind the counter.

"I will."

Maro hurried out the front door. Bastard was still standing at the post as if hitched, and his ears quirked upon seeing his master. The scent of a bakery mingled with the copious mounds of street manure, and if hunger tickled Maro's gut, it didn't now. Ambling to the horse's side, he patted his neck and spoke in low, soothing tones.

"What do you say you sit this next one out, old timer? Going hunting for a monster, and it might be better to let the missus take this quest."

Bastard knickered in response, craning his neck in the direction of the town stable.

"Yeah, you can get fat and bored while I'm gone. Maybe a sugar cube or two?"

Bastard's head swung back in his direction, and he nuzzled his rider.

"Yeah, you're a good boy—when you want something."

Maro led the horse down the road. Once at the stable, he unsaddled Bastard, brushed him out, put him in his stall, and fed him oats and hay. Once he saw to Bastard, he went to the other stall where his mare awaited. She was a dark beauty, black as midnight, and larger than most; she had to be a giant herself to support Maro's frame without him dragging his feet. Standing over seventeen hands high, he'd worked with her and Bastard at the same time, trying to make her accustomed to him and his commands. Bastard might be ornery at times, but he took orders. Maro's new ride seemed … resistant.

"We're going out for a few days. You ready?"

She twitched her ears and stared at him.

"Not very expressive yet, are we?"

Again, he got nothing.

"What a bitch."

He sighed and walked out of the stable, grabbing his bag.

At the hovel he called home, he threw his bag on the rumpled bed, did a slow turn to take in the dilapidated surroundings of a water-stained floor, peeling paint on the walls, the stale smell of dirt and mold, and the milky white windows.

Well, that's depressing as shit.

So, he headed right back out.

I need to hire a cleaning lady.

But that meant spending more money, and right now, even with all the work he pulled in, he treaded water. He needed a big payout to change his life, and if such a windfall came his way, he'd leave Tepress behind—woes worthy of a drink, but he didn't consume anymore. He'd been tempted when Runnel offered him spirits, but he had the constitution to resist.

There were several taverns in the town, but only one where bounty hunters gathered. At one point, it had an elegant name, or so the stories went. Now *The Hormoans* was scrawled across the board. Maro thought it'd be better to spell it right. People might assume only ignorant wretches frequented there, but everyone enjoyed the play on words. Indeed, hormones ran wild, and at any given time, you could hear a whore moan.

He entered the saloon, parting the swinging double doors. Smoke lulled through the air, an entity unto itself. Sweet and spicy notes hung thick, carried from the kitchen's simmering pot. The noise hit him, and all with subtle tones: conversation, laughter, the jingle of coin, the ruffling of playing cards, drinks picked up or set down on the table, and some stooped, broke-back sod tickling the ivories.

Why don't they ever call it the piano obsidians?

The inside resembled a hunter's cabin, or that's the impression he got. He'd never been in one before. The wood slats in the floor were unfinished, sanded down by patron traffic. Animal heads clung to the walls, most the docile kind of wildlife: deer, a fox, a bear, two wolves, and a mountain lion. Again, they were the docile ones. None were a warg or any of the other monsters lurking all over Atar. That he knew; he was the only sorry bastard in this joint who'd killed one.

He entered the flow of moving patrons as he scanned the room, searching for Bloodbane, and found him sitting at a table to the left and in the middle of a throng of tables. A Sional sat with him. The back of the dark complected man faced Maro, but even so, he stood out. A shock of white hair crowned him.

Pushing through the people, Maro made his way over to the glossy wood table, pulled out a brass and crimson chair, and sat.

The dark-skinned Sional glanced at him, his movement sharp and quick, then his eyes went to Bloodbane.

"Don't worry," Runnel said in his thick accent, "friend for job."

25

"Indeed?" the Sional queried in a smooth voice.

His eyebrows shot up over pale violet eyes, the incredulity on his clean-shaven face quite blatant. Had his tone been a fabric, Maro would've guessed it silk, not that he'd ever had anything so fine in his life.

The Sional held out his hand.

"Ciacus."

Maro took his hand and shook it. "Maro. What kind of name is See-uh-cuss?"

Ciacus gave a brittle smile. "My kind."

Maro shrugged. "Fair enough, I suppose." He regarded Runnel. "What's the word?"

Bloodbane grimaced and leaned forward. "Extortion."

Maro's eyes slid to Ciacus and back. "Someone else taking a slice of the pie?"

Ciacus laughed. It was rich and saturating, like a thick spread of butter on warm bread. "By the Autarch, no! I don't hunt."

Maro scrutinized the man, noting he didn't have any visible scars. Come to think of it, he had nice clothes, too. "So, what do you do?"

"I equip hunters with the best instruments."

Maro grunted. "Don't we get that at the guild hall?"

Ciacus laughed again. "I'm sorry. Did he tell you nothing about me?"

Maro shook his head.

"Well, that's disappointing. Yes, you get your wares from them. Fine specimens, too, but I make them exceptional."

"How so?"

"I augment them, make them more. Take this, for instance …" Ciacus reached into the bag sitting in the fourth chair and produced a metal bracer. It landed on the table with a metallic thud. He reached back in and pulled out a matching one for the other arm. Along the sides were metal fins, and razor sharp by the looks of them. Everything about the bracer was black, except the fine edges of the fins, which were silver.

Maro shrugged, his finger fiddling with the nearest sharp, protruding blade. "What am I supposed to do with this?"

"It's protection, for when you get up close with the creature, and trust me, you'll be up close to the danger when it has its maw around your throat."

"Don't lie," Bloodbane cut-in. "I have plan."

Ciacus smiled. "Well, let's hope it doesn't include dying." He turned his attention back to Maro. "When whatever you hunt is pressing down on you, and their glistening fangs are so close you can feel its hot breath, you'll be thankful for the bracers."

"So, I hit them with it?" Maro asked.

"No, you push it up into their chest. The palladium will do the rest."

Maro latched onto the word. "Palladium?"

Ciacus nodded. "The fine edges are rimmed with it. Press the fin into their flesh, and the palladium, right here," he said, pointing with a finger to the silver edge, "will go to work."

"And what exactly's the palladium doing?"

Runnel answered, "Depends on beast. Sometimes, they act drunk, or fall, can't breathe."

"Or sometimes," Ciacus added, "it enrages them. Either way, they lose their strength and most of their abilities, but it makes them dangerous when they're trying to flee."

Maro mulled over what Ciacus imparted, then his eyes went to Runnel.

"So, how's he extorting you?"

Bloodbane waved his hand to the modified bracers. "Four-hundred crowns! He thief!"

Maro gazed at the bracers. The expensive palladium aside, the bracers appeared to be of cheaper quality. Maro's philosophy was if you were going to buy something, make it top-quality. It'd last longer, and he'd get more use out of it. During his time with the army, they didn't buy the finest equipment; everything broke, and they had to replace it almost immediately.

Military grade's a coded phrase for shiny shit, but turds can't be polished.

On the other hand, having something half-assed on this outing might save his life. He still didn't know what kind of creature they were hunting, and some special expensive metal was better than none.

I need to save up for a sword. Too many creatures come in close for the kill.

"I've got two hundred," Maro broke into the silence. "I can pay for one now, and pay for the other later."

Ciacus chuckled and shook his head. "No bargain. They're a pair."

"Yeah, a pair of shitty bracers," Maro countered. "Ain't no one going to buy that shit. I assume you made it for Runnel. He's not buying, not at the price you're asking. I am. Some money's better than none."

"True," Ciacus conceded. He pointed a finger at Runnel. "But if I sweat him long enough, he'll cave. I've got all the time in the world."

"I don't," Bloodbane countered. "We leave tomorrow."

Ciacus shrugged.

"So, how about it?" Maro pressed.

Ciacus sighed and rolled his eyes. "Which one's your good arm?"

"My right."

"Okay, I'll sell you the left one."

"What good's that going to do me?"

"It's not, but if your arm gets ripped off, you still have one to make money with, and I'll still expect you to buy the other one."

Maro didn't argue with the man's logic. If he didn't have but the one arm, what was the point in buying the other?

"Fine." Maro forked over two hundred crowns, and his purse felt empty.

"Pleasure doing business with you," Ciacus said as he scooped up his earnings. "You won't be disappointed with the product. If something's damaged, I'll fix it for free the first time. After that, there's a small fee."

"Why so generous?" Maro asked, the hairs on the back of his neck rising. "You expect something to go wrong?"

"Not at all," Ciacus countered while shaking his head. He stood. "But even the best musket has a misfire. I prefer repeat business, and outfitting customers over and over's far more profitable than trying to drum up new clients who don't know me. My reputation spreads by word of mouth. I take care of you, and you will take care of me."

Valid.

"Prosperous hunting," the Sional said, and he departed.

Maro glanced over at his fellow traveler. "Shall we retire for the night?"

Bloodbane nodded. "I want another tumble. You should have, too. Ten crowns for the best!"

Maro eyed the room. It had been a long while since he laid with a woman, and the last time he did so was to remove his curse. He inspected his fingers, but the familiar blue-black that marked the accumulation wasn't there, so there wasn't a reason to visit one of their … hostesses yet.

Ten crowns. Autarch's breath! Is this guy trying to bleed me dry?

Maro shook his head.

Bloodbane shrugged, took another swig of his ale, and passed the rest to Maro. "Don't be late. Stables, dawn."

With that, Runnel lumbered off.

Maro's eyes went to the little swig of ale left in the glass. A sigh escaped him as he pushed it away, got to his feet, and left the saloon to return to the depressing shit hole he called home.

Chapter 3: Animals And Monsters

Instinct is the preservation I've given you; where your eyes deceive you, and your heart misleads you, when your mind rationalizes, and your soul is worn down, trust in this feeling, as sure as the stars that shine above—The Book of Balance, The Sacral Compendium.

Runnel pointed up and to the left. "We camp."

Thank the Autarch, 'cause I lost feeling in my ass hours ago.

Maro had been trailing the man's wagon all day as they headed south over the countryside. Little passed between them, and he was content with that. He preferred solitude, and a quiet partner suited him fine, allowed for deeper insight into the foreigner, lagging behind.

Maro eyed Runnel's belongings inside the horse-drawn vehicle. Two massive casks tucked up against the seat, held in place by rough spun rope, not the fine, steer-herding brand. The bounty hunter had seen those kegs before, and they usually housed ale, but he doubted Bloodbane brought a hundred gallons with him.

He can't be that much of a lush, can he?

The Mium also had several smaller crates and chests, all meticulously covered with canvas and tied down. The weathered wagon, by time and use, still held great condition, a testament that the foreigner took care of it. At this rate, he'd go another two decades before replacing the wood.

The man's well-organized. Too bad the army didn't learn a thing about orderliness.

Well, that wasn't true. Their orderliness sprinkled in shovel-fulls of chaos. But Maro knew a thing or two about men like him: their disposition made them controlling, getting what they wanted, bossy or not.

That's why he keeps asking about my saddle.

No wasn't an answer in the foreigner's vocabulary. And even if the bastard managed to make Maro cave, he wouldn't be happy for long, nor would the Mium respect him.

He's kinda like a woman. Can't respect a man who changes for her; that's why I'll always stick to my guns.

Maro shifted the reins to guide his young mare to their new destination for the evening. She ignored his guidance—more of a suggestion—and continued along the trail.

"Whoa, girl. I want to go this way."

Her head dipped, but she didn't alter course.

"Alright, Bitch. You're young, but you'll break before I do."

A snort punctuated his statement, but he couldn't tell if she communicated or whether it was just random chance. Either way, she proved as stubborn as a jackass, and did so in quiet defiance, the telltale heehaw absent from their battle of wills.

It took him longer to join Runnel than he would've liked, but he got there after doling out a few choice words, a strong arm, and a few swift heels into the flanks.

After tying her to a cedar tree and hobbling her—*that'll teach the bitch!*—he pulled his gear from her back and set to grooming. Rule one on the trail: take care of your animal and your equipment before yourself.

The army taught him that, and it still proved true. Men lost beasts of burden, had weapon misfires, and equipment malfunctions because they were too concerned with their gut and feet than actual necessities that kept them alive.

Finished, Maro dropped his saddle on the ground with a muffled thump, took off his hat, and wiped his sweating brow with the sleeve of his gray coat. It'd served him well, the garment, ever since he picked it up on the plains while chasing down the Lanton gang.

His eyes swept over the sloping hills that lined the right side of their southward trek, some with jagged ridges, all with crevices and ravines too numerous to count. Stone and shrubs peppered the jutting landscape like zits on the ass. South and to the left side of their path, rolling plains were broken up by the tall, willowy grass and clumps of trees in the deeper portions of the landscape. What little forestry that grew sprouted tall and wild, the pubes of Atar. From a quick glance, most were cedar with a smattering of firs. And like salt adding flavor to a dish, massive oaks sprinkled into the mix, often standing alone and larger than life.

Or maybe they're ash considering how massive they are.

He shrugged his shoulders. It's not like he could tell from a hundred meters away.

Replacing the hat back on his head, he bent to rummage through his pack. Runnel was doing the same over by his wagon, but Maro noted the man would dig through a crate or chest, then close it or cover it back up in a tidy fashion. It might stem from mistrust, but he doubted it. People like Bloodbane were creatures of habit, and Maro liked the trait about the other bounty hunter. The ex-soldier had his own patterns, to an extent, but without being psychotic about it.

The sun had almost slipped below the red horizon, and after a full day of travel, what they hunted still remained a mystery. Was that intentional on Runnel's part, or did he not think about such things? It was time to broach the subject. He couldn't get a read on the Mium, but a little chat, perhaps some philosophizing, and everything might wash down like hot, early morning coffee.

Or I could end up not liking him and be tempted to put a bullet in his head.

The thought soured in Maro's stomach.

"Nice coat," Bloodbane said from behind him.

Still bent over his pack, Maro glimpsed the man out of the corner of his eye. "Ain't for sale."

Runnel chuckled and ran fingers through his beard, pulling it out long and untangling the curls. "All's for sale, even morals."

Maro contemplated for a moment. His initial gut reaction was a refute, but while in the army, he let them erode a bit for a slice of compound interest to his soul.

"Not anymore."

Runnel nodded as he sat on the ground. "Good." He held up a finger. "One day, you do again. What will you do?"

Maro straightened without finding whatever the hell he was looking for. He kind of forgot now, what with Runnel talking and Maro trying to decipher his strange accent and his broken speech.

"I guess shoot whatever's making the problem."

Bloodbane laughed. "You funny man, Maro! I like you." His laughter died, and he spread his arms wide, glancing around. "Not everything be shot."

Maro shrugged. "Worked so far."

Another chuckle. "You see? That's why you come! I sad when you die."

Maro's spine stiffened. "Pardon?"

Uh, ain't you supposed to keep it a secret about killing someone?

The Mium sighed, his left hand untangling the unruly mop on his face. "You die on hunt. Don't worry, I try to save, but don't hope."

"Well, that's fucking comforting." He swallowed. "What're we hunting, anyway?"

"Offod," Bloodbane said, scarcely above a whisper.

In profile, Maro could see a bitterness etched on his features. And then, it was gone.

"A what, now?"

"Offod; their name. Sorry, my tongue. They copy you, a mimic, a cackle."

"I'm lost."

Bloodbane frowned, thinking. "Crocotta? Not nice."

Maro didn't say anything, letting the man talk. He ambled around their budding campsite, searching for rocks to form a campfire ring, and kindling to feed it. He bent to pluck a stone from the ground and tossed it into the area between him and Bloodbane, noting the man sat on his ass with no intention of budging.

"Nasty," Runnel mused, scratching the left side of his head. "Come in twos."

Another twig, another rock, both tossed. "Pairs? Why did you call them mimics?"

"They mock you, laugh, taunt."

By now, he had enough rocks to build the meager ring, so he went to the center of their possessions, squatted, and assembled the circle of stones. Now that he thought about it, whenever Maro wasn't trying his damnedest to understand him, Runnel's accent softened, and he understood easier.

Runnel sighed. "They vanish."

Maro squinted at him as he spoke. "How so?"

"Like scaled bug on twig."

"A chameleon?"

"Yes, chameleon. Can't see them; tear into you."

Shit; sounds horrible.

"Any weakness?"

The Mium shrugged. "Turning, er—move direction. Too fast."

What in the Autarch is he saying?

He let the words tumble in his head while he worked, trying to make sense of the jumble. Stones in place, Maro stacked the twigs. With his flint and steel, he could create a spark, and that'd be all he needed to let his boon take over and make a flame. "Too fast? Can they outrun us?"

Runnel nodded.

"A horse?"

"Too easy."

Well, my chances of survival are diminishing.

Maro tried to think of what might be faster than a horse. There were plenty of animals in the world of Atar; he just never cared to know them all. It's not like they were all local. He knew plenty about serpents, but that's because they gave him the heebie-jeebies. The term phobia didn't describe his visceral reaction, and there were only three: freeze up, blind rage, or run like the Cursed chased him. Most of the time, it was freeze or run, but the blind rage was something he'd learned about himself in the army.

His fellow soldiers caught wind of his fear, and they thought it'd be funny to bring a grass snake into his tent one night. He would've killed the kid had others not been there to pull him off. The serpent in question squirmed away as Maro tore up the tent, bashing the young soldier.

Should've broken his jaw.

"One chance," Runnel said, breaking into Maro's thoughts, "be close. Behind ear, stab with knife—not deep—mimic freeze. Keep blade there."

Yeah, just get close and stab behind the ear. Don't worry about the sharp teeth trying to bite you.

Maro grunted.

"So, what makes them monsters and not animals like everything else?" He stood, walked to his pack, and pulled his flint and steel from within.

As he returned to the kindling, Runnel spoke, "Good question. You have mind for hunt. Animals hunt, breed, and eat all but Atarian. Some, yes, but rare. Monsters hunt anything, you, me, horse." He shook his head. "They have power. Mimic copies laughter; a siren copies real p-person. Person? This correct word?"

"People."

Bloodbane gave a single nod.

"Sirens not Atarians. Not like you and me." He sighed and rubbed at both temples with one hand, hiding his eyes for a few moments. "Atarians are monsters."

Ain't that the fucking truth?

Maro struck the steel against flint; a shower of bright sparks bloomed in the night. With his boon, he grasped three and engorged them into flames. With absolute control, the fire burned hot, catching onto the twigs he'd gathered.

"*Oju kayan*," Runnel whispered.

Maro frowned. "What now?"

"You have fire boon!"

"Half. Just aspects."

"Half's better than none!"

In terms of a boon's tiers, Maro sat in the middle, called aspects. The highest, those who could call flame into existence, were adepts. The bottom rung, those without much of a gift and unable to manipulate elements, were regulated to the affinity level.

"I suppose. What's yours?"

Bloodbane came forward, holding his hands near the flames. "Water."

"That's helpful."

The other shook his head.

"I'm thirsty, always. If no bath or swim, I grow sick, weak." He waved a hand back to the wagon. "That's why I bring barrels."

Maro glanced over his shoulder. He'd been wondering what was in the enormous casks, but he hadn't wanted to pry.

"Both are filled with water?"

Runnel nodded. "I get pot and meat. You cook dinner, yes?"

Maro nodded, and when Bloodbane turned away, he rolled his eyes. He supposed he couldn't complain too much. Bloodbane was taking him under his wing and letting him get his first taste of hunting monsters. Before long, Maro hoped to be chasing down hags, sirens, harpies, and whatever else he could kill. He didn't want to be so green that he'd end up dying while chasing coin.

Runnel dropped his stone-gray pack at his feet and tossed a new shovel with his other.

Maro's eyes tracked to the fresh tool, remembering the conversations he had with Horace and Drallus. "What's the shovel for?"

Runnel's gaze went to the wooden haft, and he shrugged. "Just me, I wouldn't bring."

"So, what's it for?"

Bloodbane rubbed his belly. "Two reasons: we dig hole for shit, and I bury you."

Man's got my death pretty well planned out. Wonder if I should be worried or just put a hole in his skull.

"You seem to be counting on my death a lot."

"Odds, not personal."

Feels pretty fucking personal.

"Course not."

Bloodbane continued, "Each hunt, you grow wise, less chance to die. This ... eh ... is caution. That right word?"

"Precaution."

Bloodbane cocked an eyebrow and glared at Maro. "Yes, precaution. Unless you want to feed birds and beasts?"

Maro shook his head.

"Good, now, cook supper."

As Maro prepared the meal, the Mium set his portion of the camp to how he liked it. Part of this included configuring some form of hanging bed under his wagon, suspended from the axles, and well off the ground. He thought the man both a genius and ludicrous.

When asked why, Runnel pointed to the sky. "Rain comes."

Maro grunted and glanced at the emerging stars. There were some heavier clouds rolling in from far off, but he wasn't a weatherman. He thought about calling the pale Mium out on his bullshit. It'd been a dry winter, after all, and they were starving for rain, everything from the rivers, to the grass and the beasts.

"You sure?"

Runnel laughed. "Huh huh huh. You chance the rain? Go ahead. I stay dry."

Well, that's that. Who'd know better about the rain coming than someone with the boon of water?

By now, the ex-soldier came to understand some of the cadence to Runnel's speech. Being a stranger to the land and language, Maro suspected the man's vocabulary was more extensive than he expressed, but why use twenty words when four sufficed? The more the foreigner talked, the more his sentences varied, but it wasn't by much.

Meal prepped, a stew with salted venison and potatoes, they sat down to eat, and Maro returned to their conversation regarding boons as they ate.

"So, what can you do with the boon of water?"

Bloodbane shrugged, then spoke around a mouthful of food. "Much like fire. Heat up, cool down, make ice, or steam."

"Can you?"

"No. My skills ... different."

"Such as?"

"Wonder about my name? Bloodbane? Not normal back home." The man sighed. "Blood is water of body; ancestors cure town of blood sickness. Very useful."

Maro took another bite, this time chewing slower.

By the Autarch, something that powerful ... to think what someone could do with it!

"Not all family was ... er ... decent," Runnel continued. "Great uncle killed a man."

Maro swallowed. "How?"

Runnel, who'd been holding his bowl near his mouth as he shoveled his food, lowered it until his arms rested on the insides of his legs.

"Pulled out his blood."

Maro felt his stomach drop out at the declaration, and he went cold all over. That sense all battle-hardened veterans get in the calm before a gun fight, when they sense the wrongness of the moment ... yeah, that settled over him right now. All of what Horace said tumbled in his mind again—the group of fighters went out with Bloodbane, and they didn't come back. They were experienced hunters, and here he was, eating a meal with the man and ready to sing around the campfire.

Fuck.

"Fool did it in town," Bloodbane commented. "Ever since, family is Bloodbane."

By the Autarch! I don't have to watch for a gun or knife; he can yank out my blood!

"No one cares about rule," Runnel supplied, "only ception."

"Huh?"

"Ception. No one cares about rule, only ception."

"Oh, exception."

Runnel nodded, then locked eyes with him.

"People focus on one time, not when saved from death. Our name, it is bane."

Maro swallowed a small spoon of stew.

"So, why keep it? You're in a new place."

His eyes roved over the foreigner and the tangle on his face.

"Why not call yourself Runnel Blackbeard?"

"Are you Maro Stick?"

Asshole's got a point.

"Yeah, but ain't Blackbeard more menacing?"

"Is stick scary?" Runnel shook his head. "It's not curse." He thumped his chest. "Badge of honor. You crazy people love my name."

Better than Prakk.

"I've heard some," Runnel continued, "breathe under water."

He made swimming motions with his arms, still holding his bowl in one hand, thumb hooked over the wooden spoon so it wouldn't fly out.

"Can you?"

The foreigner shook his head.

Maro's mind flashed back to some of the darker times with the army.

That'd come in handy during torture sessions and replicated drowning.

An owl hooted in the distance, drawing his attention to the night. Another owl took up its call, followed closely by a third.

Three? Never heard that before; then again, I've never paid the wildlife much attention. It was covering our tracks at night while we scouted or slept in the bush.

There was another kind of bush he wanted to scout out, but he couldn't afford to spend ten crowns for it.

Maro glanced out into the darkness, seeing if he could spy the winged predator perched on a branch. As he scanned, in the distance and on the ground, something moved. His skin tingled. The movement had been two quick blurs, one right after the other, or at least he thought so. Did the night play tricks on the eyes? He blinked, unsure of what he saw, if anything.

Maybe I imagined it? With Runnel's story and all, perhaps I'm a tad jumpy?

"What?" Runnel asked.

He shook his head. "Might be seeing things."

But Maro doubted it; deep in his core, his gut warned him, and his eyes never betrayed him. At least, not during the night. In daylight was another matter entirely. Would he listen, or let his rational mind assuage him? But the eyes didn't lie, not his anyway. He could see at night better than in the day, where he contended with the bright glare, and his eyes ached from squinting, but without the sun, the shadows were his to command.

"No," Bloodbane said. "*Crocotta.*" The older bounty hunter belched. "You good cook, Maro. You come more hunts."

"Hmm, what's that now?"

"Good cook."

"No, the other part. You said it's the 'crocotta'? The mimic?"

Runnel shrugged. "We close; they roam for food."

Ice poured down Maro's spine, and his head snapped back to the open area where he'd seen the movement.

Right now, we might look like a tasty treat.

"Damn the Autarch, why didn't you tell me?"

Bloodbane eyed him from his seat, shoveling another heaping spoonful into his mouth.

Despite Runnel's words, what Maro's eyes saw, he couldn't be sure. In fact, it might've been tall grass swaying in the distance, a flicker of shadows in moonlight, the shiver of trees in the wind. Animals were easier prey than two bounty hunters.

He hoped.

The nagging feeling wouldn't abate, and his scalp tingled. Maro set his dish aside and stood, wading away from the fire and deeper into the darkness where the woods, wildlife, and wind kept him company.

"You shit?" Runnel called after him, laughing his familiar huh huh huh. "Don't forget shovel!"

Maro scanned the immediate surroundings, listening, watching. He lowered his hands to his side, pulling the trench coat behind his holster. The other hand twitched closer to the massive hunting knife on his left hip. The shadows revealed their secrets; nothing remained hidden from those born with the boon of fire. A possum nosed around the trunk of a tree; he caught sight of one of the hooting owls from earlier perched high above it, its eyes large and dark, and the shadows danced in the moonlight.

While he and others like him enjoyed the rarity of getting sick, immune to almost all poisons, and commanding all aspects of flames, the other half of the boon—the absence of light—yielded to their control: deepening shadows or piercing them. Sometimes, Maro thought the boon wasn't worth it, not when he suffered from perpetual coldness, light sensitivity, and weakness in the sun. Brittle bones and lack of body strength rounded off the drawbacks, not to mention his rail-thin figure no amount of food would sate or cure, not even animal fats, dairy, or sweet cakes.

"Hey," Runnel called again. "Shovel."

"I ain't gonna shit!"

Maro's eyes drifted to the middle of the field, in the tall, willowy grass, the area where he noted movement earlier. Had it been his imagination? The serenade of crickets came to life like a maestro on strings.

His gaze roved the ground and vegetation not a few paces away. A rabbit hopped along, causing the owl to swivel its head. It took off, its flapping wings silent, honing in on its next meal. Branches rocked with the gusting breeze, a flitting tree critter dashing from limb to limb.

Otherwise, nothing stirred.

His hands tingled, the way they used to right before the shooting started and an advancing enemy charged his position. It made his asshole pucker, too. For some ungodly reason, his mouth went terribly dry.

But he knew what he saw, two distinct movements, low to the ground and quick. But low was relative, and from his vantage point of sitting, they could be larger than initially thought. Whatever the movement was, it was too small and quick to be a bear; too quiet, too. Besides, he hadn't heard of any this far south, but anything could happen. Not long ago, a warg almost tore out his throat.

"What?" Runnel called from by the fire.

Still, that pent up energy, the bated breath, didn't fade. Maybe he was going crazy? Maro shook his head.

"I wanted to make sure."

As he turned back, he tripped over a root sticking out of the ground. He stumbled forward but kept his feet. Bloodbane gave a hearty chuckle.

"Huh huh huh."

"Ain't that damn funny," Maro said through gritted teeth.

By the Autarch, why'd he have to be an asshole?

Maro glared at him as Runnel stood, his face slack.

"That wasn't me."

Maro's gut tightened, and he cast his eyes behind him, his hand going for the musket-pistol on his hip.

"Fuck."

Goosebumps riddled his flesh, and the hairs on the back of his neck stood on end.

Runnel came to his side with a noisy sigh.

"Long night. Give me gun. I watch first."

Chapter 4: That's What I Sound Like?

Though beasts may rise, or hordes travel in packs, no number is too great for you, for I have made you supreme in the land—The Book of Law, The Sacral Compendium

Maro sat huddled in his dark grey coat, pulling it tight against the dropping temperature. Clouds rolled in while he slept, and from the looks of it, the Autarch wasn't done making a shitty situation worse. The winter had been dry, the last rain months ago, and now as it warmed up, here came a cold snap.

Any moment now, he's going to piss on me, the insufferable little shit.

A drizzle would make an already miserable Maro more unbearable, but he doubted a light sprinkle awaited him. It didn't help his perpetual state of coldness, and sitting here, shivering in his boots while the sky drenched him, wasn't appealing. It reminded him too much of his time in the army.

Bloodbane let him sleep first, and the apprehension of handing over his weapon while slumbering didn't bring the best rest. Had it been any other situation, a refusal would be in order. With the mimic so close that Maro mistook it for a genuine chuckle made his asshole clench tighter than trying to hurry to the privy at night. The way he saw it, if he died by Bloodbane's hands while he slept, it beat having his throat torn out by some animal.

He wouldn't have brought me just to kill me.

A soft rumble overhead prepared Maro for the worst—nothing more terrible than being cold, unless you added water to the situation. A gust of wind kicked up, causing the trees to sway with an angry hiss like a swarm of distant hornets. He wrapped his arms around his chest, tucking each hand into the pits of his opposite arms.

Damn you, Autarch; you must really hate my ass.

And if the Everlasting Autarch did, Maro could blame no one but himself. Did the Almighty have some running joke, or did fate have a sick sense of humor? Maro's time in the army had been some of the worst experiences in life: exhausted, sleep-deprived, terrified, cold, wet, with people allowing strange fungus to grow on their feet. Every day brought another dice roll to see if you lived, or what other afflictions plagued you. Maro found himself profoundly grateful no rot grew on his nut sack, not like that poor kid, McNeily, who bitched and whined every day. He refused to change or wash his underwear because he thought they were lucky.

The man survives one firefight, and he attributed it to his shit-stained drawers.

Maro felt sorry for the kid, but more troubled by what became of him; however, his demerit of intolerance wouldn't allow for such sentiments. McNeily's stupidity got him in the end, and when the healers finally made their rounds, castration only staved off the inevitable.

Ain't no way to live.

Maro shook his head, closing his eyes while the chilly wind numbed his face.

McNeily lay screaming until someone felt pity enough to feed him a musket ball. When the smoke cleared, no one thought less of the man who pulled the trigger, and Maro never knew who'd done the deed. He didn't want to. The official reports said McNeily shot himself because he couldn't bear the pain anymore.

He grunted.

Without a reason to go on, I'd shoot myself.

He'd made many mistakes in life, and not insisting on McNeily's hygiene was one of them, but he couldn't decide for people. Each had their own lives, and he could only hope they did their best. Advice was marvelous—when you asked for it. Otherwise, it festered like an irritant.

Maro glanced at the snoring bounty hunter under his wagon, amazed to find him wedged between the undercarriage and the suspended pallet. Bloodbane was a mound underneath, a log between the two axles.

This brought a chuckle to Maro, but he stifled it so as to not wake him.

He turned away, gazing out over the tall grass and wild oaks. The cedar trees tangled through the vegetation like Runnel's untamed beard. Maro let his mind drift to his childhood, anything to take his mind off the monotony of keeping watch, and to keep his thoughts from drifting back to McNeily, but it didn't work.

Thinking about McNeily soured his mood. When he'd been younger, his uncle, Cosanto, his mother's brother, told him about a monster called an ekayu. As a little boy, he could never remember the name, so his uncle told him it was the butt monster. If Maro didn't behave, the ekayu would come out of the darkness and bite him on the butt.

For the next half-year, his poor mother watched him prowl around the house, holding his cheeks, making sure no monster came within striking distance. His mother, being a devout woman, prayed for him, not knowing the cause of such brash behavior, and their religious order, the House of Lust and Candor, told her not to worry, that he'd grow into a fine follower and produce many offspring.

I'm thinking those holy men are full of shit. No kids, and no woman to tango with, and I ain't been to the holy house in I don't know how long.

A single splash against the brim of Maro's black hat broke into his thoughts. He shifted his shoulders, his eyes scanning the darkness.

"Shit," he muttered to himself.

And here it comes, the rain, the Autarch's way of pissing on me, and showing how little he cares for my wellbeing.

Of course, if Maro became a god, he'd do a lot worse than bringing thunderstorms. Knowing his temperament, he'd drive people insane. And if no one could resist his power ... he let the sentiments die.

Damn good thing I ain't a god.

His eyes swept left to right as the singular droplets picked up, becoming a slight drizzle. Now, out there in the darkness, everything moved. Almost every tree limb rocked up and down as the water hit the branches, and with the gusts of wind, they moved back and forth. They were like monsters coming alive, stuck in the ground because dirt and rock covered their feet. He glanced at Bloodbane. The Mium still slept in that contraption. As long as it didn't flood, he'd stay dry.

Lucky bastard.

Drallus's warning and Horace's words still caused Maro to doubt Runnel's intentions, not to mention the shovel, a strange tool for a hunt, but maybe Bloodbane spoke the truth? Did the Mium intend to bury him should he die?

You're going to be disappointed. I don't kill easy, and I refuse to die until I'm good and ready to give up the ghost.

The precipitation came heavier now, and Maro took a quick peek skyward. Water splashed on his cheeks and got into his eyes. He blinked to clear the water.

The Autarch's making it easy for him, freezing me to death.

Maro, still holding his arms to his chest, uncrossed his right hand and reached for the fire, coaxing the flames higher. The heat washed over him for a brief second before they returned to their normal size. He didn't want to manipulate it too much, otherwise the Curse would start on the tips of his fingers. Having the boons such as fire, water, and life also meant you had to contend with the curses. Too much of the corruption, and you'd turn into the Cursed. His uncle, Cosanto, didn't need to tell him about the ekayu, not when real life bogeymen existed.

And anyone of us could become them. That ain't something they teach in school.

Getting to his feet, he snagged a log from the pile they'd stacked before turning in. Wood placed, Maro grabbed his pack and set it over the remaining logs.

Won't do to have soaked wood. I'll have to play with the flames to keep it going.

As he turned back to his sitting spot, another movement shifted at the corner of his vision. He froze. His head snapped to the right, where the movement had been. The tall grass moved, but he couldn't see anything. That creeping chill came back; it rolled down his arms. Maro squinted, willing the shadows to melt away, but nothing manifested. The swaying grass kicked up by the wind made it impossible to be sure.

"Hmm."

Was it an animal, the wind, or the mimic? A tension pricked the space between his shoulder blades, like the tip of the knife ready to plunge through his soft skin. Remaining still, his eyes did the roving, a frantic, darting search of the trees, the grass, the spaces between shrubs, and the darkness blanketing it all.

Nothing.

But the quiet … that foretold what he couldn't detect. He took a deep breath through his nose, staring intently into the night. The oh-so-cold hand of trepidation slipped beneath his skin and held his belly like a man holding the swelling womb of a lover. The hairs on the back of his neck stood, and no amount of logical, self-recrimination alleviated the sensation.

"Get it together," he whispered to himself.

Tight bands encircled his chest, making it difficult to breathe. His hand shook from the cold, not the fear—at least, that's what he told himself. His flesh blossomed with a fresh ripple of goosebumps.

And then, he heard it: a grunt.

His grunt.

Shit, that's what I sound like?

The mimic had to be close enough to hear him, and considering the quietness of such a sound, he might've been right up on him. His scalp tingled at the thought. The mimic could've been a single pounce away from tearing out his back. His heart fluttered, realizing how close death had come, and turned away.

Unless they have god-like hearing.

Runnel hadn't covered that aspect. Or perhaps he didn't know? Either way, the thought settled into his gut as comfortably as a red-hot poker searing his insides.

Maro heard his grunt again. His eyes shifted to the tall grass in front of him. The towering stalks swayed in a sudden gale, but not quite strong enough to howl.

That'll come soon enough.

An owl hooted again, copied by two others. A ticking sound followed, like something coming from the back of the throat, a slow croak, the beginnings of forming a word.

Shit, shit, shit.

Chill aside, and numb fingers, his hands shook all the more.

Not terrified, not terrified, just the sudden urge to shit, that's all.

He knew this feeling well. It happened before all battles, when bullets started flying and people were dying, screaming out agony to their god, that's when the body said, 'Oh, lovely time to shit or piss or vomit,' while your mind wrestled with the ludicrous reaction.

Maro hobbled backwards, never taking his eyes off the grass. Now that he moved, he could feel the coldness in his legs. The wind and rain tossed the foliage in sporadic whims. A steady bead dribbled from the brim of his hat, dripping past his eyes. The back of his boots hit something, and he glanced down.

The wood pile.

Eyes back to the front, Maro reached for his bag sitting atop the stack with this left hand, rummaging for the bracer he bought from Ciacus. The metal brushed his fingers, pricked the tips, and he pulled it out, clamping it around his left forearm and outside his coat. At his right hip, he still had his single-shot pistol, but he didn't plan to draw it until certain of this target. By then, it might be too late.

Not that it'd do anything.

Or would it?

Bloodbane's chuckle sounded from his left, and Maro snapped his head in that direction.

What the hell?

Followed by his grunt to the front.

His eyes went back to that spot.

Shit, both of them.

"Wha's tha'," Runnel's thick, sleepy accent called from under the wagon.

"Mimics," Maro said, his voice grating after so many hours of disuse. "Get your fat ass up."

The thunder crackled overhead with a mighty boom. If the mimics made any more sound, those precious seconds drowned it out.

"Huh huh huh," came Bloodbane's deep belly laugh, but it still emanated from Maro's left.

Maro's grunt, "Hmm," came from the front.

"Fuck." Maro said.

"Fuck," one echoed back.

"Huh huh huh."

An ungodly, piercing howl came from the both of them. The screech was painful, enough to make Maro wince and cover his ears. Pain pierced him to his teeth, like when he ate snow or ice the first time. The horses whined in terror, and Maro spared a quick glance at the tethered Bitch. She stirred, trying to look around as he moved.

By the Autarch, that stings! He rubbed the nub of his ear.

Maro slipped his left hand to his belt, pulling his serrated knife from its sheath. Maro knew warfare, and these intimidation tactics meant only one thing. An imminent attack was coming; now, the mimics had to talk themselves into it—so to speak.

"They come now," Runnel said from somewhere behind him.

Yeah, no shit. Maro's eyes darted left, right, and center, frantic to see any sign that might give him a moment of warning.

"Huh huh huh," cackled one.

"Huh huh huh," echoed the other.

His breath came fast through the nose and out of his mouth. He whispered, hyping himself for the coming battle.

"Come on, you sons of bitches!"

By now, Runnel had crawled out from under the wagon, and his footfalls placed him just behind Maro; the end of a long barrel musket poked out past Maro, and he caught a glimpse in his peripheral vision.

"Come, you dogs!" Runnel shouted.

"Uhh …"

That isn't the smartest idea.

"They think twice," Runnel explained. "Now, two of us and them. By yourself, hunger makes them bold, but two?" He shook his head. "I think not."

"There's one ahead of me," Maro said, dipping his hat in that direction. The water flowed off the brim in a rush like a miniature waterfall. "Another to the left."

"Bitch is mine."

Runnel aimed his musket to the left, and the cocking of the hammer filled Maro's ears. For a single, nostalgic moment, Maro was back with Jeb during those years with the army.

Guns, rain, colder than dirt, and fucking terrified; it's like I never left.

Maybe that's why the bounty hunter gig drew Maro in, a familiar touch he couldn't turn away, why he wanted to track monsters.

Send a monster to catch one.

"Mine," the mimic to the left repeated.

"Bitch," came from the front. "Hmm."

"Fuck." Again, back to the left.

"Maybe we should expand our vocabulary?" Maro muttered.

"I like. Simple."

"We're at a stalemate. Something's got to give."

"Very well."

Bloodbane fired his one shot. The sudden explosion of fire, gunpowder, and metal was deafening.

A yelp rose from the grass.

Did the bastard hit one?

From the front, the 'huh huh huh' faded, as if the creature retreated.

Maro let out a breath he didn't know he'd been holding. The rustle of grass grew fainter as the beasts fled, but the wind and downpour picked it right back up. He couldn't be sure they'd left.

A feint?

"Good shot, I think," Runnel congratulated himself.

"I'd reload if I were you."

"No."

Bloodbane shook his head in two quick motions.

Damn the Autarch, why do I always get saddled with the halfwits?

"In this weather? Wet powder will misfire."

Okay, yeah, he's got a point, but it ain't like I want him to stick the barrel up in the sky during a torrential downpour.

Some of the tension from earlier eased out of Maro's shoulders, and he turned to face the other bounty hunter. Runnel stood half naked—the top portion.

Thank the Autarch for holy miracles.

His gut swelled out like he carried a child, and rain beat against his pale, so terribly pale, moon-lit skin. It hurt Maro's eyes.

"Damn the Autarch," he said. "Should use you in a lighthouse."

Bloodbane let out his belly-filled laugh. "You funny man, Maro."

Had Maro not been watching him, he would've thought the mimics had returned. "You've said that before."

Runnel shrugged. "It's true." He shot fingers through the unruly tangle of his soaked beard. "Gods, feels good! Be happy! Hope it rains whole time."

Knowing the Autarch, he'd do that to spite my ass.

"Ain't you cold?"

"No." Runnel rubbed his belly, smiling with a malicious grin, but Maro thought his stomach more like a waterskin filled with honey. "I keep warm. Maybe you need fat?"

Maro twisted his lips and suppressed a grunt. With the crocottas out there, he didn't need to give them something more to copy.

Runnel ran his fingers through his curly, tangled locks, and now that the water added weight to the mess, it extended down to the middle of his back rather than hovering around his collar.

"Glorious!" said the big man. He smacked Maro on the chest with the back of his hand. "Agreed?"

Maro shook his head.

"That's your problem," Runnel said, wagging his finger. "You don't enjoy moments. That's story's moral: life is moments. You see one big thing."

"I'll remind you to 'enjoy the moment' when those mimics are ripping your balls off."

Runnel chuckled. "No matter how bad, could be worse."

Now you've done it.

"I don't know," Maro answered, "that's pretty bad." He cast a glance at Bloodbane. "No more women."

That sobered him for a moment, but with a shrug, Runnel said, "Could be dead."

Without the aspect of enjoying the finer things in life, or having a family, I'd rather be in the ground.

But he wouldn't voice those thoughts to Runnel. Besides thinking him touched in the head, Bloodbane might let Maro die.

Let's not give him any motivation to refrain.

Another crackle of thunder came overhead, and a flash of lightning lit up the night, causing Maro to close his eyes in pain. In that moment of vulnerability, half-blind and head searing with pain, he heard it.

The sounds of footfalls reached his ringing ears. Rustling of grass caused him to spin around and pull his pistol. The telltale snap of swaying branches made him scan the trees. Runnel reacted, too, aiming his musket towards the sounds.

What the hell are you going to do with that? Damn thing ain't loaded!

Just as the thunder rumbled overhead again, something came crashing from the woods, sliding across the mud-slicked earth. As it neared them, Maro sighted down the barrel, aiming for the head sliding to a stop at his feet. He almost pulled the trigger.

Staring up at him, first in terror, then in surprise, was a woman.

Chapter 5: Atine's Reservoir

Men, cast your gaze upon a woman and take pleasure from the sight, for I have made her image to be the foil to even the greatest of hunters, and a nurturer, like your mother, before your mate entered your life. Women, stake your future upon a man you deem as a prize, for I have made him capable of being your protector, provider, and leader, as was your father, before your mate came into your life—The Book of Obedience, The Sacral Compendium.

"Who the fuck are you?" Maro asked. He gazed down the barrel of his gun, the bead still centered over her face. The rain came pouring down, splashing against the back of his neck, the droplets pattering against her dark face. A steady waterfall dripped down the barrel of his gun, splashing against her forehead.

"Katya," she said in a breathless voice.

It took a moment for him to breathe, to realize she wasn't a threat.

"A Sional?" Runnel asked, and by the sound of his voice, he was just as shocked as Maro. Sionals kept to their homeland on the other side of Atar, or they congregated in cities. Few traveled far from their homelands that spanned mountainous terrain, swamp-covered jungles, charred-broiled deserts, and breezy coastal plains. Katya's hair was dark, helped by the rain, though Maro could've sworn he noted red undertones.

Maybe it's the feeble firelight? He glanced at the camp. *No, too far away.* He turned back to her.

Her eyes were on the darker shade of mauve, a grayish tinge coming through the purple.

Ciacus, the Sional that sold Maro the bracer, was an exception to the rule; finding the man in a small town had been the exception, and now Katya made a pair within two days.

"What are you doing stumbling around in the dark?"

She blinked a few times; the droplets filled her eyes. "Mind if I get up?"

"Yes," Maro answered, but she ignored him and stood anyway.

Why'd you even ask?

Maro didn't holster the musket-pistol, but he lowered it to his side. Out of the corner of his eye, Runnel shifted his stance, an inattentive hand rubbing his belly.

Yeah, makes you wish you put a shirt on, don't it? Nothing like a woman to make you reevaluate your physical flaws.

Dwelling on such things with mimics nearby seemed counterintuitive. But men thought in terms of physical attractiveness, and Maro was pretty sure Bloodbane could claim to be prettier, as long as a woman didn't mind the kettle around his gut, or a shaggy cat fucking his neck.

"What are you doing out here?" Maro inquired again. The thunder rumbled overhead, and he could've sworn it got a lot colder in the last few moments.

Katya shrugged. "What business of it is yours?"

He cocked an eyebrow.

"Well, how stupid do you have to be to go running through the woods at night? There are people with guns, trigger-happy travelers, and monsters lurking about."

She rolled her eyes. "Lucky for me, you're only a monster."

Maro grunted.

She might have a point.

"What Maro means—" Runnel began in his thick accent.

But Katya cut him off, "Huh? I can't understand you."

"—dangerous," Runnel finished.

"What? Dangerous? Where's your sense of adventure?"

Maro could think of a lot of things that were adventurous: playing cards with armed, drunk citizens; riding an angry bull with nowhere to run; catching a coach to the ass-end of nowhere … but crashing through vegetation while the gods pissed on you in the icy darkness wasn't on the list.

"Alright," Maro said, nodding as he spoke. "Have a good one."

Both Katya and Bloodbane jerked their heads in his direction.

In unison, both blurted, "What?"

He holstered his gun. "You want adventure?" He waved out to the wilderness. "Go on. Watch out for the crocottas."

"The cro-what now?" she asked.

"Don't worry; it'll be fun. An adventure."

He turned and started walking back to the fire.

"Maro?" Bloodbane called. "What you doing?"

"Respecting her wishes. It's what she wants," he said over his shoulder.

Once he reached the fire, he squatted and tickled the flames with his boon, causing the flames to leap over three feet high. He closed his eyes and winced.

Damn, that was stupid.

But he couldn't help it; he was cold and soaked. Soon, the shakes would set in. A sudden wash of heat swept over him.

Ah, that feels wonderful.

"You have the boon of fire!" Katya gasped, coming forward with hurried steps. She held her hands out, drinking in the warmth.

Maro looked up as she entered the circle of light and heat.

"Hey, you wanted adventure, right? Go run around in the dark, make your own fire, catch your own food. Since you think I'm a monster, go play with the real ones."

"Maro!" Bloodbane admonished. "Don't treat ladies so."

"She's not a lady," he countered, centering his gaze upon his partner. "She's a stranger who refuses to answer simple questions. In my experience, that's a fast way to die. Woman or not, she can slit your throat as easily as the next bloke. So, she ain't welcomed until I'm satisfied."

"Really?" Katya asked. "You'd do that to me?"

Maro turned his head at a ponderous pace, glancing up at her.

"Damn right. You'll get no special favors from me, and if more men were smart enough, they'd be doing it, too."

"What experience?" Runnel mocked. "You green, never hunted monsters."

"Hmm. New to the profession, but ain't new to killing. I've got five years with the army, the basilisk dragoons. I fought on the Eastern Front of the Redinar Wild Lands in the Barren Frontier, and I survived the worst of it."

"Oh," Runnel said, sounding deflated. "Special hell."

Maro grunted.

Yeah, even you wouldn't want to go.

Maro overheard officers saying the mortality rate sat near seventy-two percent. With those kinds of numbers, rumors were bound to circulate.

"Okay, fine," Katya said, squatting down beside him. "If I tell you, will you let me stay?"

"Depends if I think you're telling the truth."

She paused for a moment. "Fair enough. I'm out here hunting for Atine's Reservoir."

Runnel laughed, slapping his knee. "So stupid."

Maro glanced between the two.

"What the hell's that?"

Katya's lips thinned in irritation, but Runnel spoke. "Atine's Reservoir, a myth."

"It's not a myth," Katya retorted. "I'm close! I know I am!"

"You think," Runnel continued, "he buried treasure out here? Middle of nowhere?"

"Can you think of a better place?" she countered.

"Too easy!" Runnel said with a chuckle. "Two dozen. Even drunk, I can name five."

She nodded, and by her expression, irritation and indignation burned within her.

"Alright, name them."

"What?"

"Name them!"

Runnel paused, cocking his head to the side. "Gastur's Tier."

Katya nodded.

"The best minds and treasure hunters have combed it over at least a dozen times."

"Pikovides?"

"Been there myself, and archeologists have cleaned the ancient city out, not to mention thieves."

"Well—"

"Sorry to cut into y'alls' geological jaunt," Maro interjected, "but this has no bearing on her right now, nor does it solve the problem of the crocottas."

She eyed him, narrowing her eyes.

"You said that earlier. What are they?"

"They're beasts."

"Monsters," Runnel corrected.

She focused on Bloodbane.

"I'm sorry; what's your name?"

"Runnel. Runnel Bloodbane."

"And you're a Mium, right?"

He dipped his head in acknowledgement.

"I've never seen one of you."

Runnel smiled, a thimble of color coming to his cheeks; or maybe the firelight caused it.

"Meeting Sional is rare treat."

"If you two are done with your mating ritual," Maro interrupted, "I'd like to get on with the story."

Katya's head whipped back around to him. "Are you always this cheerful?"

"Nah, just intolerant to bullshit."

She nodded. "Makes sense that's your demerit."

"Yeah? And what's yours? Carelessness?"

She smirked. "Adventure. Can't find one sitting at home."

I could. I mean, digging around in your sock drawer and finding two without holes in them is a miracle.

Lightning flickered in the distance, followed by a rumble. Maro took a quick peek skyward. Clouds were supposed to keep the warmer air trapped, but with the rain and the dropping temperature, snow wouldn't surprise him.

But this deep into spring?

"Hmm. Well, that's one I ain't never heard: adventure."

"I know! I'm unique! Now, tell me about this monster."

Maro shrugged. "Bloodbane knows more, but they paid us a visit right before you showed up, which is why I greeted you with the business end of my pistol."

"What do they look like?"

"Didn't show themselves, but I can tell you what they sound like: us."

Katya stood, stepping closer to the fire. Maro's eyes roamed over her. She was a damn fine-looking woman, just his type: fit and lean, her build honed by rigorous hours on the trail. The rain-soaked clothes left little to the imagination. Another notion struck him. Maybe that's what she wanted by stepping closer to the fire, to distract from her part of the conversation. He realized he'd interrupted their discourse about some treasure, and she never returned to it.

That's kind of smart ... and duplicitous.

"What House are you from?" he asked, an uneasy feeling settling over him. He dreaded the answer.

"Deceit and Compassion," she answered without hesitation.

Well, there ya go. Stumbled across a girl who's gonna lie her ass off to you, but she'll be benevolent about it.

Now that he thought about it, how was she any different from all the other women he'd met?

She'll be better at it.

He shook his head. He didn't have time to think about that now. Women were a distant figment, and he'd never entertained the notion of settling down with one other than having a child of his own.

In a world this botched, am I good or evil to bring a child into it?

"Well, that's unhelpful," Katya said, breaking into his thoughts, "not being able to tell me what they look like."

Maro pulled his soaked coat tighter around him and fought like mad not to shiver.

Runnel took over, explaining the finer details of the beasts they hunted. Through his flirtatious meanderings, Maro learned a few more irrelevant details: the mimics were a hybrid between mountain lions and wolves, predatory features of both despite looking more like an overgrown dog. In a lot of ways, by the details, they looked like a miniature warg, and Maro knew those beasts well enough, having killed one with fire nine months ago. Each crocotta had a different color coat, and you'd never know until they were dead, since they shifted to blend into their surroundings.

That means these creatures are on four legs, and if I was a smart man, I'd listen to Drallus's advice and high-tail it out of here.

But Maro also learned a little about Katya during the exchange. Despite Runnel's obliviousness to her distance and subtle cues, she wasn't interested in him in the slightest, and at a guess, it wouldn't deter Bloodbane at all.

When Runnel's ramblings drew to a close, Maro spoke, "Well, I ain't getting any more sleep tonight, and it's too damn cold, anyhow."

"Agreed," Runnel said.

"Yeah," Katya echoed, "I don't think I can sleep in this weather either."

Uh, who the fuck invited you?

"You sleep in my cot," Runnel offered. "It's dry, with furs to keep you warm."

Katya presented an insincere smile. "My clothes are soaked, and I'd ruin your dry cot."

Unperturbed, Runnel offered, "I have clothes. You change."

"Well, if Maro isn't sleeping, and neither are you, I don't want to hold up the party. We can start the hunt tonight."

Maro squinted in confusion and glanced up.

"What's with this 'we' shit? You're not a bounty hunter, and I don't remember inviting you."

Katya rounded on him, turning her backside to the fire. Good thing, too, cause he'd been staring the whole time the other two had been talking.

"Are you assuming I'm not a bounty hunter?"

"Yeah."

"Are you?" Runnel inquired.

"And what if I am?" she countered.

Maro stood.

Water sloshed off his hat. It didn't keep him from getting his head wet, but it kept most of the rain getting in his eyes, and his scalp a touch warmer than his hands, but not as ice cold as his crotch or toes.

"Then, I'd say show me your bounty hunter chit."

"Chit?"

"Yes," Runnel added. "Every hunter has."

"I don't," she confessed.

"Then, you ain't a bounty hunter," Maro finished.

"Just because—"

With a wave of the hand, Maro cut her off.

"Did you pay your guild dues?"

She held up her hands.

"Fine, I'm not a bounty hunter, but I still want to travel with you."

He shook his head. "Sorry, sweetheart, I ain't allowing you to take my cut of the prize."

She shrugged. "Fine, but when I find the treasure, you're not getting a cut of mine."

He smirked. He didn't believe a treasure existed, but if it did, he doubted she'd find it.

"I like that arrangement. Besides, you just want to travel with us cause it's safer in numbers. I hope you got supplies, 'cause you ain't getting mine."

Now that he thought about it, she had nothing with her.

What's she really doing out here?

Katya waved her hand out into the wilderness.

"I left my stuff back at my campsite. We can stop by and collect it."

Oh, we can, can we?

"What brought you to us, anyhow?" Maro asked.

"The gunshot, of course."

Runnel took a step forward.

"You hear shot, and run to it?"

She nodded. "Muskets are single fire use, and judging by the sound, you were close enough that if I ran here, I could arrive before you reloaded."

"What if there'd been more than one person?" Maro asked. Judging by her face, she hadn't thought of that.

"You don't like me much, do you?"

He shrugged. "You haven't given me a reason to."

"I like you," Runnel said from behind her. "Come, you ride in wagon. We huddle for warmth."

Runnel turned, headed for the wagon. Katya gave Maro one last glance, resignation mixed with something else, as she followed.

Maro glanced at the fire.

Yeah, don't worry about it, I'll kill the flames. Cozy on up for a free wagon ride.

Chapter 6: One Too Many Mouths

There is no greater evil than a proud soul who refuses to surrender; there is no greater good than a humble soul who refuses to accept defeat—The Book of Balance, The Sacral Compendium.

`

The rain still poured down, and the cold snap riddled his brittle bones with pain—the Autarch's way of punishing Maro for every foul thought conjured. Or maybe he relieved himself at Maro's expense. Dampening his soul and souring his mood came as a bonus.

Must have a huge bladder.

And that didn't account for the clinging chill. His teeth rattled together, a shiver to rival the patter of a tapper's feet on the dance floor. His breath plumed before him, and with each exhale of fog, he ached, knowing how much heat left him.

The ground beneath Bitch moved in a steady flow, a constant stream of liquified mud, tumbling rocks, and drowning leaves.

Soon, we'll just swim to the mimics' home.

He tried to keep up a vigil, his eyes roaming the bushes, the edges of the path before him, searching for any sign of the monsters, but his misery cut through his focus like sharpened steel through taut rope. Once frayed, it'd never be whole again.

The downpour had worsened in the last hour. Maro pulled his coat tighter, left hand holding the top closed, not that it made a damn bit of difference. The principle mattered. He crossed his arms again, stabbing himself with the bracer for the twentieth time.

In all honesty, his mood darkened with each plodding step Bitch took. She reeked, and that meant he smelled like a dozen eggs left in the outhouse for a week. He was tired, hungry, wet, cold, and if he rode much longer, his soaked britches would chafe the skin right off his inner thighs, not to mention the two small lakes pooling in his boots. His socks might spawn tadpoles in the brewing swamp water.

A coldness burrowed into him, one Maro hadn't known in a long while, but it returned as if an old companion. His feet turned frigid and pruned as the precursor to frost turned into a serious worry. He couldn't feel his toes for the last hour, and in the last few minutes, his breath started pluming before his face. A throb filled his boots, similar to—what he imagined—a hammer taken to his tender lower extremities. An ache stabbed his small bones, a sharp blade of misery digging in like a zealous dentist searching for festering teeth.

Lightning flickered overhead, revealing the turmoil in the sky for a terse moment. Staring at the ground kept him from going blind, and the terrain turned rocky with a gentle incline, which meant less mud, but not much.

Less chance of injury, too. I'll take small miracles where they come.

Runnel's laugh reached Maro's ears, and he glanced in that direction. Up ahead, Runnel and Katya sat huddled together on the swaying wagon, no doubt warmer than he, sharing some type of canvas. In fact, he doubted Bloodbane was cold at all.

The ex-soldier hadn't even asked about Katya's boon, but it's not like people walked around proclaiming it. No, it was more akin to men visiting whorehouses; they didn't parade around town announcing their visits—unless saddled with the Bloodbane name. Sure, some arrogant swines touted their gifts, used it as an extension of their personality, but those types of people were scarce.

Thunder rumbled, and Maro imagined the Everlasting Autarch clearing his throat, ready to boom out his voice from the heavens. Up ahead, watching Runnel and Katya laugh and talk without a care or discomfort made him reevaluate all he hated in life: the storming squall above, the gods, the damn cold, and their newest guest.

Guest? What guest? She barged in like we ought to accept her. Damn woman.

Part of him wanted to give her a piece of his mind, the other half just wanted to give her a piece of him—the one that counted.

Fat chance, Sticks. By the Autarch, how long has it been?

Long enough.

It always happened the same way, caught between anger roused by a woman, and the arousal she coaxed out of him. He'd rely on the angry treatment: the safest, cleanest, and easiest to maintain distance and clarity. Women had a way of clouding his mind. While Maro might've noticed all the signs that Katya wasn't interested in Bloodbane, she hadn't shown him anything, either.

I'm too damn blind to see them if she did.

The lightning flashed again, and for a moment, Maro wondered if the storm was moving away. The clouds swirling above them in a circular pattern told him everything he needed to know, and a few things he wished it didn't. At times, the wind-driven rain came at them sideways, peppering his face.

It's just going to hover up there and shit all over me until I die.

A splash pulled Maro from his internal irritations, and Bitch lurched underneath him.

"Easy, girl. Slow and steady."

Traveling at night was downright ludicrous. The horses could hurt themselves, break a leg, or the wagon could snap a spoke or two. And it made seeing the monsters all the harder. Could they be out there right now? His eyes darted out, searching for any sign, his chest tightening with worry.

Who had this fucking bright idea, anyway?

Maro thought back. What he could recall, he only said he wouldn't sleep anymore, but nothing about traveling. And now, he'd no idea of their destination.

"Hey!" he shouted. "Where are we going?"

Katya glanced back, a smile fading from her face in the lantern light, a confused expression replacing it. Between the wind and precipitation, she clearly couldn't hear him from ten paces away, let alone the distance that separated them. He could scarcely make out the details of their huddled forms.

Well, that's just great. She's up there having a grand ole time, staying safe and warm, and I'm out here freezing, terrorized by what I can't see.

The trees swayed again, tall, dark, and terrifying things. The way they shivered, the sound of groaning branches, spoke of a story entrapping him. They leaned over and loomed, a shady canopy in the day, but skeletal hands that reached for them at night. His eyes went back to Katya, who'd faced the front again.

Fat lot of help that did me.

Maro kept his eyes on the trail. It widened a touch now, and in the distance, the ground rolled in sweeping hills.

Fucking great. Just what we need.

The thunder rumbled again, a testament to the dark presence of the Almighty Autarch glaring down at him.

Hills meant mud slicks, impassible with a wagon laden with water barrels, not accounting for Runnel's size or gear. At least a rifle or two, a shovel to bury Maro with, a couple of changes of clothes, some food...

He needed a wagon for all that?

A tiny load, minus the water barrels, of course. In fact, Maro carried almost as much during the army. His pack held boots, clothes, food, water skins, while he carried his musket. It didn't take a team of horses to move them.

But if they'd given us a wagon, we would've dumped that shit off and found more to carry.

The thought made him think of his own horse. Maro wanted to feel sorry for Bitch, but found himself grateful he let Bastard stay behind.

Rippling puddles reflected the flickering light above as lightning crashed again.

Bloodbane cackled again. "Huh huh huh."

That son of a bitch—

A growl, a flash of movement, and an impact threw Maro from the saddle.

He landed on the ground with a thud; the wind rushing from his lungs. Water splashed everywhere, getting into his mouth and eyes. Bitch screamed, kicking her hind legs up twice, then bolted. Maro blinked the stars out of his vision, and he sucked in a wheezing breath.

What happened?

He sucked another breath, his lungs burning. He gasped. The fog cleared, but not the panic.

"Fuck," he heard, followed by another cackle.

The hairs on the back of his neck stood on end. He came to his knees, glancing around. A cedar stood watch nearby, a slab of rock tearing through the flesh of the earth, scattered shrubs too small to hide something the size he expected, muddy ruts in the ground. His eyes went up to the tree, watching the swaying limbs. They were all moving, but was it the wind, or the mimic?

And the rain still poured.

A deep, throaty growl was all the warning he had.

From the rock, the beast lurched. Maro never saw it. Another impact threw him on his back, the weight of a boulder on his chest. He jerked his arms up to protect his face. A flash of teeth came for him. The beast clamped down on his arm and yelped. The weight receded, vanished, and Maro scrambled to his knees, coming face to face with the monster.

It stood less than five feet away. Its black lips peeled back, revealing bloody fangs.

Shit! Is that blood from me?

He couldn't feel anything, but the adrenaline didn't give him time for an inspection. His hand slipped to the gun at his waist.

A long snout edged closer, the fur rippling, changing color from a wet-soaked brown to the damp caliche of the rock face behind the creature, to the blackness of night. Its eyes were dark, a color Maro couldn't make out. And it was bigger than a wolf.

But not as big as a warg.

The lips peeled back, its maw opening. The tongue looked blue, but it was hard to tell with water in his eyes.

"You gonna kiss me with that mouth?"

The growl rose, as did the shoulder blades.

"Come here, bitch. I got something you can deep throat."

Maro jerked his pistol, cocked the hammer, and pulled the trigger.

Nothing happened.

"Shit!"

The crocotta jumped, and once again, Maro found himself on his back. A sharp pain ripped into him as the teeth punctured his chest.

"Fuck!" he screamed. Putrid, hot decay washed over him. He swallowed a mouthful of the creature's breath. The urge to vomit was almost more powerful than the terror. He had to survive, had to do anything. Claws scrapped against his shirt and belly, digging a hole in Maro's stomach, searching for a bloody snack. Sheer seconds separated life from death.

In desperation, he swung his right hand. The pistol connected with the mimic's head with a thud that reverberated through them both. A yelp from metal and wood on bone was the only reprieve. Less than two heartbeats, the terror ensued again.

Teeth nipped at his pectoral, his body jerking, his shirt tearing. Maro wailed on the beast. Once, twice, three times. On the fourth, the monster latched onto his arm. Fangs pierced coat, shirt, and flesh. His skin exploded with the heat of punctured flesh and blood.

The agony was unbearable, the stench unimaginable, the searing of lacerated flesh. He screamed and thrashed, screamed and kicked, and screamed some more. The mimic dragged him across the road by the arm, digging into him, the clamping power constricting like a dead man's noose. Maro's throat ached from rawness, his voiced terror, pain given vocalization.

The monster tugged at him, wrestled him through the muddy terrain, breaking for the woods. Sharp rocks stabbed into Maro's back while the incisors skewered his body. With his left arm, he clubbed the animal, hitting, bashing, pounding for all his worth, praying to the gods the bastard let him go. And then, the sweet rapture of bliss as the maw opened.

The crocotta spun, mouth agape, but this time, it dove for Maro's throat. Maro reacted without thinking. With his left arm, he braced for the inevitable. As the canines closed around his throat, the creature's body rocked into him, his left arm wedged between them. Before it ripped Maro's soft flesh open, the monster yelped and jerked away. Blood trailed down the creature's chest and belly, puncture wounds weeping down its wet coat.

It shuddered and took a tentative step forward. Its colors shifted through numerous hues at a flicking pace, black, stone gray, tan, foliage green, brown, a rustic red, and in between, parts of the animal seemed to disappear from view, blending in with the background behind it. In the lull, Maro still couldn't get a decent look at it.

What's happening?

Maro glanced at his left arm still cradled against him, noting the bracer, the fins coated in blood. Then, everything clicked. The palladium. Ciacus had saved Maro's life.

Damn! I'm buying all my shit from that Sional from now on!

"You fucking bitch!" Maro growled.

Somehow, during the attack, Maro kept control of his pistol. It stopped the initial attack. He knew it wouldn't work, but it'd make him feel better, maybe buy him time. And if the Autarch would grant one miracle, it'd be that.

He feared he ran out of favors or divine intervention when he rescued Maribel.

He cocked the hammer again, took aim, and pulled the trigger. The sound of the shot echoed out, and the crocotta squealed and thrashed, nipped at the air, and retreated, stumbling over bush and shrubs as it hurried away.

Confused, Maro glanced at his pistol. The smell of gunpowder curled through the air, but no smoke wafted from the end of his barrel.

"Maro!" Katya shouted.

With the attack over, the adrenaline fled, leaving him weak of limb. He collapsed to the ground.

Why in the hell is it so cold?

Katya came bolting to his side. She slid on her knees across the muddy, slick ground. "Are you okay?"

Maro shook like a trembling leaf, then let his head fall back. Whether from the cold, the terror, or both, he couldn't say.

"I think I shit myself."

He tried to hand her the pistol, but the shakes increased, and his body trembled with fatigue. She grabbed hold of it.

"It's okay, I've got you," she said.

Maro couldn't tell if it was the rain or not, but it looked like she was crying.

Don't weep over me.

Heat and cold flashed through him.

"Maro!" Runnel's distant voice called out.

Save yourselves, fools.

Maro reached up to grip Katya by the shirt, to pull her close, to whisper his last words, but he didn't have the strength, and he only groped her breasts.

Not bad for my last act.

"Bury my ass."

Whatever strength remained fled, and the impatient embrace of death clawed at his soul, and after a vile life weighed with regret, he was ready to surrender.

Chapter 7: Close Encounters Of The Naked Kind

Let the touch of a woman arouse you, heal you, and temper you; by her hand, she is commanded to nurture you. Let the touch of a man gratify you, guide you, and protect you; by his hand, he is commanded to provide for you—The Sacred Texts, from The House of Lust and Candor.

When Maro opened his eyes, the stabbing firelight made him wince, and his mood soured and settled somewhere between surprised and pissed. He'd planned on meeting the Autarch and giving that cantankerous bastard a swift kick in the ass for all the bullshit he put Maro through. It'd been a hell of a rough life with no sign of reprieve, but if he had to wake up after being mauled half to death, Katya's face wasn't a bad way to come back into the world.

Her skin was smooth and clean, and her cheekbones were not as pronounced as he once thought. Her long, graceful neck reflected firelight, the hollow casting a deep shadow. His gaze roved lower before he caught himself; her eyes, up close, were wide and expressive, and he drowned in her mauve and gray pools that twinkled with mirth.

She smiled, and the skin around her eyes crinkled with delight. "There you are," she said, her voice soft. Her fingers ran through his short brown hair. "I feared you wouldn't recover. It's almost like your soul wants to leave."

Through the fog of his mind, he digested the words, trying to make sense of them. About that time, he realized multiple things: his head lay in her lap, his face pressed against her bare breasts, a rough texture rubbed against his stiff member, signaling he was naked.

"Gods' wrath!" he croaked. Heat rushed into his face, and he tried to move, but she pulled him back against her naked chest.

"None of that; we're almost done."

"With what?"

"Healing you," she said. Her voice held a puzzled tone, and her brow mirrored the emotion. "Never been healed before?"

He grunted. "Yeah, but they weren't naked."

Her shoulders shifted in a miniscule shrug. "It's the way I've always done it." She gave him a playful smile. "You've got a blanket covering you, but thank you for the compliment."

His brow drew down as he gazed into her eyes. Only the Autarch knew how much he wanted to lower his pointed stare, but he realized what she meant, and a whole new heat flushed his cheeks.

By the gods, it's not a soldier I can command to stand down.

He thought of anything to say, to drag his mind off her, to draw attention away … Bloodbane, Bastard, the rain, the crocottas.

"A cultural thing?" he blurted.

She shook her head. "I'm not gifted much with the boon of Life. Plenty of people are much stronger than me. They can heal wounds with no scarring. I need skin to skin contact for it to work, and the more, the better. With your wounds, I didn't want to take any chances."

Damn, the first time she takes off her clothes for me, I wasn't awake to enjoy it.

A sudden realization hit Maro.

"You got naked around Bloodbane?"

She chuckled. "No, I sent him out to watch and listen for any more of those creatures."

"In the downpour?"

Katya shrugged again. "He seems to like it."

"Hmm. Boon of water."

"Really? Those are most revered in my land, especially those who dwell on the doorstep of the desert."

At the mention of water, Maro realized none splashed his face. He cast his gaze up, noting a rock wall above them. With his eyes and not much movement, he surveyed their surroundings. The limestone walls held a glint to them, and water clutched to the stone. Though dim, it wasn't dark, and that either meant the fire was massive, or they weren't deep inside. Judging by the pouring outside, they were near the mouth.

"Where the hell are we?"

"In a cave Runnel found."

How'd he manage that in the pouring rain? Guess those with the water boon have a few tricks up their sleeves.

He was grateful to be out of the downpour, and that Katya brought him back from the brink.

"How long?"

"A few hours. Dawn's fast approaching." She went silent for a few moments, and in a quieter, reluctant voice, she said, "I'm sorry. I can't make the scars go away. The attack looked worse than … well, it's beyond my abilities."

He frowned and hefted his right arm, the one mauled by the crocotta. Bite marks trailed up the skin on both the top and bottom. Some were small, but others were as big as the pinky's fingernail. A few jagged lines remained where his flesh tore. He remembered his chest, and he glanced down. Red lines trailed down his stomach in a V-shape where the beast clawed at him, but the flesh was whole and an angry pink.

Maro grunted. "Well, at least it'll distract from my face."

Katya chuckled. "Your face isn't so bad. It has character."

"Oh yeah? Where?"

"Did you know your nose's a little crooked, to the left?"

"Yeah, broke it."

"I take it the pockmarks on your right cheek are from a childhood sickness?"

He absentmindedly touched it. "Yeah."

"And that's why you have the shadow of stubble, to hide it?"

He gave a single, truncated nod. When she didn't say anything else, he spoke, "You forgot about the hard lines in the forehead."

"That's because I think nothing about them. It gives you a rugged appearance."

"My face looks a hard forty, almost double the years I've been alive."

She stroked her fingers through his hair again. "Maybe, but you look better than most men in my country. Beauty's the veneer obscuring the soul, and yours is beautiful."

Incertitude smothered his features.

"You've been drinking Bloodbane's spirits?"

She laughed, the whites of her teeth bright in the gloomy cavern and flickering firelight.

"No, but I can tell. I have a way of seeing what matters."

"And what do you see?"

He almost feared what she'd say.

68

"Your bluster and crass behavior's a mask for caring. When I look into your eyes, I see the shadows haunting them, the dimness of your light, and that's not something you'd wish on anyone."

Fucking ouch. How the hell can she tell?

"And Bloodbane?"

She shook her head.

"He's not what he wants you to believe … hides a lot, and there's little of importance other than his own desires. That man would've strapped me across a barrel, if he had his way."

Maro chuckled.

"Perhaps you *do* have a gift."

She echoed his mirth.

"Which's why I tried my damnedest to save you! You can't leave me alone with him."

He heard the unspoken words, the worry in her voice, and he tried to diffuse her anxiety.

"Well, I tried, gave the creature ample opportunity, but I'm like toughened leather."

She smiled.

"I can tell."

"So, what'd you do? Strip down and lay on top of me?"

She shook her head, and her soft, dark hair with red undertones tickled his face, and he imagined that's what silk felt like.

"For my health and safety, I hugged you from behind. Didn't want to get stabbed while I healed you."

"Gods' wrath, woman! Kick a man when he's down, why don't you?"

She dipped her head, and her gaze roved down his body.

"Or when he's up."

"Son of a bitch!" Maro rolled to the side, his back to the frigid wall, and he bundled the blanket around his shoulders. It itched to hell and back, demons puncturing his skin.

Katya chuckled and extricated herself. She stepped in front of him, reaching for her clothes. As she did, he glanced up, taking a moment to admire.

Guess it's true what the good book says: a woman's figure's medicine for the soul.

69

Bundling her clothes in her hands, she waded deeper into the tunnel for privacy.

Smart idea.

As she walked, he noted her lithe form and the muscle tone. The gods spent time chiseling her out of marble, a fine masterpiece.

Damn, make that two people who can kick my ass: Katya and Bloodbane.

While she left, he dressed. In haste, he climbed off his makeshift bedroll and glanced around for his clothes. He found them sitting around the fire. Snagging them up, he dragged his sodden, partially warm, half-cold pants up his legs, doing the familiar hop at the end to inch up that last precious amount. Wet clothes and dry skin never matched, and the temperature made him shrivel.

Damn, didn't hurt too bad. Maybe I'll survive, be a little prettier when I take my shirt off.

The ghost pangs of his injuries shot through him, tender muscles and aches; weakness loomed at the edges, threatening to return the moment his attention drifted away. Goosebumps riddled his flesh as he shrugged into the ruined shirt, still wet and cold. He thought about pulling out a new one—if they weren't soaked already, they soon would be—but thought better of it. Those beasts would end up tearing up the new one, and he didn't have many to spare.

Now clad in wet clothes, he shivered, his jaw quivering from the cold. He reached for the fire with his boon, coaxing the flames. A breath of heat hit him, but it'd never be enough to satisfy or chase the chill away.

If there were dragons, I'd tickle their crotch in payment for blasting me in flame.

He shrugged into his coat when Katya stepped back into view, her hands behind her back.

Thank the gods she's clothed! Death by distraction ain't a proper way to go, although I wouldn't complain.

"Better?" she asked.

He nodded, but he didn't know if she referred to his injuries, or finding her clothed once again. If the latter, he'd give a resounding no.

"Where's my hat?"

She pulled it out from behind her, setting it on her head. "What do you think? Payment for services rendered?"

Maro had to admit, she cut a mighty fine figure with the hat, but he chalked it up more to her garments than anything. Wet, clinging vestments worked wonders on her.

"Perhaps … once we reach the town."

She cocked an eyebrow. "Really? You'd make me wait until we got back? I want to keep the water out of my eyes."

"Me, too." A lecherous thought flitted through his head, and he took a half-step closer. Being the man he was, he spoke without a second thought. "If you're a good girl, I'll let you wear it once we're back, but that's all you'll be wearing."

Her mouth fell open, then a playful smile teased the corners of her lips.

"Not hearing a no," he said with a grin and a wink, "and even if it is, I might give it to you anyway, knowing that every time you wear it, you'll think of this moment with me."

She thought about it for a moment and gave a single nod. Reaching up, she removed the hat and lowered it onto his head. "I think it suits you."

The hurried, sloshing steps of a loping Runnel filled the cave. Maro turned to see the other bounty hunter stand just outside the entrance. Soaked, his breath fogged before him, and none of that seemed to bother him. He sucked in a deep breath, as if he'd been running a long while.

"We go. They're in cave nearby."

Katya stepped forward, and she darted a worried glance behind her. "Is it connected to this one?"

Runnel shrugged. "Don't know. I'm not mimic."

"Alright," Maro said.

But then, Runnel vanished in a flicker of motion, jerked off his feet.

Bloodbane screamed. A growl tore through the night. Lightning flashed outside. In a blink, Maro was in motion. He scrambled for the entrance, slid to a partial halt, hung a left, and found *something* ravaging Bloodbane.

Maro jerked the knife from his belt, leapt forward, and started stabbing.

"You fucking cocksucker," he growled with each thrust. The crocotta yelped with each incision, and after the first two, was trying to snap at Maro on its back. "Fucking die!"

"The ear!" Runnel screamed. "The ear!"

For a moment, it sounded like Bloodbane's accent disappeared, probably because of his screaming panic. Maro hesitated, wondering what the man was going about, but he remembered. He pulled the steel from the animal and stabbed for the ear. In a singular moment, the creature locked up, its legs stiff, and keeled over on its side.

Holy Autarch! It worked!

Runnel gained his feet a moment later, a knife materializing in his hands. He leaned over the creature. "Give me this, you sweets."

While the monster couldn't move, it could make noise, and the pain coming from its throat made Maro wince. It reminded him of all those times he heard the screams, the begging, the crying from those poor tortured individuals the army got their hands on. Maro had stood guard while they worked.

And he wasn't guiltless by half.

When he chased down the Lanton gang because they took a girl, he employed the same methods. He tortured, maimed, and killed to rescue her. The acts marred his soul, and he vowed never to do it again, or stand by while it happened.

Yes, this monster was something they were sent to kill, a danger to everyone it crossed paths with, but Runnel crossed the line.

"Bloodbane," Maro called.

"Wait. Almost got one."

"Got one, what?" Katya asked.

"Eye."

Maro reached for his gun on his hip, but he wasn't armed.

Shit.

Turning on his heel, he hurried inside.

Katya followed him, dripping a trail of water in. "What are you going to do?" she asked. "Are you going to let him torture that poor beast?"

"Hell no." He found his single-shot pistol and the supplies right beside it. Grabbing a small pouch, he tore the fibrous sack open with his teeth, then poured the powder down the short barrel. Wad over the opening, he plucked a ball from another pouch, set it on top of the wad, and used the ramrod to stuff the barrel, packing the ball against the powder. Jerking the ramrod free, his hand darted into the last belt pouch and grabbed a cap to set on the nipple.

He hurried outside, cocking the pistol. When he reached the whimpering creature, he pointed the pistol at the ear and pulled the trigger. The shot rang out like a mighty thunderclap in the darkness, only dampened by the onslaught of rain.

"What!" Runnel shouted. He stood and shoved Maro, far stronger than Maro anticipated. "What you do?"

"You were torturing the poor beast!"

"Beast? You fucking stupid!" Runnel yelled, smacking his head. "Beast tried to kill you! Kill me!"

"I didn't sign up for torture."

"You imbecile!" Runnel said, emphasizing his words with hand gestures. "No body to take back! It dissolves."

"Huh?"

"Look!" Runnel said, pointing, grabbing Maro by the collar of his coat, shoving him closer. "Already melts."

With a final shove, Bloodbane let him go.

Maro blinked a few times. *Son of a bitch. The bastard's right.*

Before his eyes, the creature was … deflating? Its essence pooled on the ground as the body shriveled. No, more than that—decomposing before his eyes, and in a few seconds, there'd be nothing left of it. He glanced back at the angry man.

"Sorry, I didn't know. Despite that, you can't—"

"Only way to get bounty!" Runnel shouted. "The eyes, most valuable."

Bloodbane wiped his face.

Maro frowned. "What about the eyes?"

"It's … superstition. Eyes harden when removed. Precious stone. They change to—er, prism. Beautiful, mystical. Some see future."

Maro smirked at that. "You expect me to believe—"

"Fool! Only way to claim bounty! You turn in eyes. Everyone knows crocotta hunts in pairs. Even if we get other, only three eyes. Three is not four! They think other escaped."

Well, shit. I fucked us hard, and not the 'hey, I'm going to enjoy this' kind.

Thunder rumbled overhead, and Maro swallowed. "I didn't know."

Runnel nodded. "No shit! You green. You fuck me! I should fuck you!"

Uh, no thanks.

"You didn't tell me!"

"No time."

Maro cocked his head to the side. "The whole day we spent traveling, and where we camped when all this shit started, you could've told me."

Runnel shook his head. "I didn't trust you. You don't drink."

"Then, why'd you ask me to accompany you?"

"I didn't; you asked!"

Maro was about to open his mouth when Katya spoke up. "Can we discuss this inside?"

Runnel shook his head. "No. We go, now. Catch bastard alone."

Maro held up his hands. "Why? What's the point? You said the contract's pretty much worthless now."

Bloodbane held up his hand, showing the prism gem that had once been an eye. "We salvage, reduced price."

So, there's money to still be made…

"Some fool will buy."

That's a cheerful thought. Wonder what he thinks about me?

Maro's eyes flickered to Katya behind Runnel's shoulder, and he caught her imperceptible nod.

"Alright; let's get the last one before it gets us."

Chapter 8: Clever

In darkness, evil spreads, beasts prowl, creatures thrive, and men sleep. I have given you fire to combat all that may come against you, for my word is the light to chase away the shadows of a dark world—The Book of Chaos, The Sacral Compendium.

The dark, cold cave stretched out in eerie silence, the kind of silence that makes the fine hairs on your arms prickle. Rain still poured outside, but within the void of shadows, a dull thrum hummed in the background, which punctuated the stillness before them. If shadows could turn tangible, a physical barrier, here's where they came to prowl.

I wish there was some kind of noise in here, then maybe my asshole wouldn't clench so damn tight.

There was noise, but not the kind he wanted. He could hear Katya and Runnel breathing, the latter loudest, perhaps because of his weight or out-of-shape stature. The same couldn't be said for Katya. He reconciled hearing their breathing to the crypt-like stillness. His shoulders tensed, and a chill shuddered through him. Was it fear, or the coolness of the cave coupled with his wet garments?

Definitely the clothes.

Maro's eyes drifted to the other bounty hunter. To say he was a slob did him an injustice. In the trio, Katya took the crown in fitness; him, the leader in combat experience; and Bloodbane, in trail wisdom. Katya, like Maro, inhaled through her nose, whereas Runnel's mouth hung agape, making it all the louder.

Does the boon of water make people mouth breathers?

Whether from the impenetrable gloom, the water beading down his back, or an actual shift in temperature, goosebumps crawled like a spider across the nape of his neck. When shivering threatened to take hold, he couldn't tell whether from the cold or genuine fear.

Yeah, prowling through a cave, no light, wet, stalking a monster that took a bite out of me, what could go wrong?

In that moment, he decided he didn't like caves. In fact, he hated them to their core, about as much as the thought of teaming up with the other two forever.

Well, she wouldn't be too bad.

The three of them could make a formidable, small unit, and equally fair, he doubted Katya had any experience in this arena, which made her the weakest link. Thinking about it, her safety was a concern and put them all in danger when he'd try to save her ass. Bloodbane would, too.

He looked her over. She had no weapons. He withdrew his pistol from the holster and passed it to her, pressing it into her hands in the darkness. She frowned down at the gun, then up at him. At least, he thought so. Too dark to tell, and his night vision only went so far, but he caught her lips twitching to speak, and Maro shook his head. He didn't know how far the sound carried in here, but at a guess, beyond the point they wanted.

Bloodbane destroyed their noise discipline a few steps later.

"Wait," the foreigner whispered, but it sounded like a shout. He knelt, pulling out two unlit torches from his belt, and struck flint to steel a few times. Maro was about to ask him what two soaked torches would do when Bloodbane glanced up at him. "Be useful, bastard."

The grizzly bounty hunter struck again. A shower of sparks glowed for a brief instant and sputtered out.

"Sorry," he grumbled in low tones. "Too fast."

A perturbed edge entered his voice. "Again."

It's not like it's a sure thing.

He struck, and the sparks exploded into view; Maro grabbed hold, coaxing the flame, drawing it to the palm of his hand. The light lit the surrounding walls. He squinted, wincing at the pain as the noonday sun kindled to life in the dark confines. Katya and Runnel bent over to pluck the torches from the ground.

When Katya straightened, her eyes went wide; she dropped the torch, aimed the pistol at Maro, and pulled the trigger.

Pain and light and the wind-ripping caress of the bullet wafted over Maro's face. A deafening explosion filled the chamber, as did a bright muzzle flash. Maro released the fire, suffocating them in darkness, and he fell to the ground, his back hitting the stone with a vibrating thud through him. His ears rang with a sonorous roar, and he clamped his hands over his ears.

Gods that hurts!

Blurred, bright lights peppered his vision. He closed them, praying for the pain to recede.

Damn the Autarch!

Maro was blind and deaf.

A crushing weight landed on him, and the wind rushed from his lungs. A second later, it leapt off, the mimic using his body as a springboard. Something inside him popped, but whether a break or just his spine cracking, he couldn't tell at the moment. The additional pain drew the focus away from his eyes and ears. He took a few deep breaths.

The faint sound of something skittering across the rock floor taunted him at the edge of awareness. He rolled to his stomach, glancing up. While they stumbled around on their hands and knees, helpless and blind, Maro tracked movement. He couldn't make out the creature in its entirety, but when shadows moved in the absence of light, it was all he needed.

"Huh huh huh," the sound echoed in the chamber.

So much for catching the creature napping.

Flint struck steel in a shower of sparks, and Maro appraised the other bounty hunter on his knees, trying to create a light.

In the tenebrous gloom, the Mium growled, "Come on, you bitch."

Maro reached for his boon, willing the embers to him. They responded, shooting through the air and forming a pillar of flame in his hand.

"Our surprise's gone," Katya said, picking herself off the ground.

What gave it away?

Katya crawled away from them, headed toward the last movement, and while dangerous, Maro couldn't help but thank her for the view.

Autarch's looking out for me after all.

"It's that way," he said, dipping his head in the direction.

"We go," Runnel said. With a scrape against the stone, he plucked up his unlit torch and held it toward Maro's flame, rolling the end through the fire, and stepped aside for Katya to do the same. When she neared, Maro stared her down.

"What?" she asked.

"You almost shot me."

"But I didn't."

"I felt the wind on my face; that's how close you were. You ever shoot a gun before?"

"No, but where's your sense of adventure?"

Not very comforting.

"The adventure," he said, his tone thick with strained patience, "is staying alive. Dead's the last stop."

And I won't ever get the chance to make you walk bowlegged.

But wisdom was knowing not to say those thoughts aloud.

She sighed. "Okay, you're right, and I'm sorry. In the future, if I shoot you, I'll make it up to you."

"How, if I'm dead?"

She shrugged.

"I'll shoot you where you can survive."

"Making it up to me better involve you and me naked, and I ain't talking the healing type."

She smiled. "Oh, that's definitely something you won't survive."

She stepped away.

That counts as flirting, right? He lifted his head toward the Autarch. *If not, at least you made her with a sense of humor.*

Maro sighed and lowered his gaze to eye her retreating figure. She paused and glanced back, a pointed look.

Way to go Maro, have her think you're staring at her ass.

"Sorry. Coming."

"Not yet."

She smiled and turned away.

Damn pervert.

The most disconcerting notion from their conversation? She'd never shot a gun before. Did she tease him, or was she being serious? No matter which way he sliced it, she'd almost killed him.

And like a moron, you handed her the means to do it.

To be fair, he didn't think she'd shoot him, let alone pull the trigger in his direction only moments later.

He grunted as he mulled over the last few minutes. Had she hit the mimic at all? They couldn't be killed with conventional weapons, not unless straight in the brain, as he had done earlier.

Damn fine thing to have a gun at your side.

And now, it was out of rounds. He'd need to reload it, and that meant extinguishing his flame. The other two had torches, and he'd call it back to him with ease. He doused it and hurried to catch up. When he drew level with Katya, he caught the pistol tucked in the front of her pants.

Lucky gun.

He reached over and plucked it from its snuggling place.

"Hey!" she hissed.

"Reloading."

What the hell are you going to do with an empty pistol, anyway?

But Maro knew. When it misfired mere hours before, he used it as a club, a life-saving move.

And almost cost me an arm.

He tore off the edge of the powder package with his teeth, filled the barrel and stuffed the wad and ball, and set the cap. An enticing thought filled Maro about stuffing it back down her britches; instead, he handed it back over, grip first.

"Thanks," she whispered.

He dipped his head in response. Reaching out a hand, he siphoned off a small bit of flame from her torch, letting it hover above his palm. Katya's eyes tracked the movement, and for a moment, she stared in fascination.

Maro leaned in close to her, his mouth almost touching her ear. She'd feel his hot breath tickle her skin; he hoped his breath didn't smell like a rotting carcass.

"Did you hit it?"

She shrugged.

Well, that's great. Almost shot for a shrug.

Bloodbane pulled away from them, and Maro stretched his legs to close the distance, finding a space halfway between the two. Thankfully, Runnel had put on a shirt and an overcoat besides. He resembled a hunched bear now. Maro kept his eyes scanning the darkness, and even with the light, it proved difficult.

These other two can't see shit.

Maro frowned, glancing behind him. Katya wasn't trailing more than four meters, but Runnel tripled that up front.

Did she hurry to catch up? Afraid of the dark?

He turned back to the front, gauging Runnel's movements. The way he moved and ducked down, darting back and forth, it was almost like he was searching for something.

He is, you idiot, the last mimic.

Bloodbane hurried a few steps over, bent, and held the torch close, only to scurry away. He dashed to the other side, holding the flame high, followed by him scampering off. By the sound behind him, Katya seemed to have closed the distance even more.

There's a monster that can eat us. Only a moron wouldn't be afraid of the dark.

He tried to think back to all their run-ins with the crocottas—in the tall grass while he'd stood watch alone, on his horse and trailing behind, and Runnel standing at the cave's mouth. The mimic couldn't have seen inside.

But this last one, they hadn't been alone. They stood clustered together. Why would it attack them while grouped?

What would I do if three people came barging into my home? I'd attack, too.

Now, however, they were spaced out, and with the Mium so far ahead ...

"Shit." He took off at a sprint right as Runnel screamed. The torch fell to the ground, illuminating the monster from underneath. It shifted colors, matching the flickering flame. Maro jerked to a halt, spun around as Katya closed the distance, and snatched the pistol out of her pants. Facing Bloodbane, Maro pulled his knife with the other hand and hurried forward.

Runnel's screams were more in terror than pain. He knew that for certain. His big fluffy coat protected him, at least for a few seconds. He'd heard many cries of agony over the years. Besides, Bloodbane cursed as much as yelled. When Maro drew close, he switched the weapons in his hands, the pistol to the left, the knife to his dominant right hand. He had one shot to get this right.

No mistakes, no pressure.

Maro cast a quick glance around, seeing massive holes in the walls that lead into darker, deeper parts of the tunnels. Sneaking up on the crocotta, he grabbed the monster by the scruff of the neck, jerked it backward, put all his weight on the yelping beast, and stabbed the knife right behind the ear. The thrashing monster stilled as Runnel climbed to his feet.

"That was terrifying," Katya said, her voice breathless.

"Beast scared me," Bloodbane said, his accent thick. "I shit myself."

Maro smirked. He had similar sentiments not too long ago.

"Wanna do the honors?"

"With pleasure."

Maro eyed the mimic on the ground. It was smaller than he remembered. As Runnel came forward, a movement drew Maro's eye, and he glanced up at the looming head of a massive crocotta, twice the size of the other two. Its lips pulled back in a snarl, the teeth as long as his fingers. Saliva dripped from its teeth and lips.

"Autarch save us," Katya breathed.

"Hmm. Ain't you a clever girl?"

It darted out of the dark hole in the wall, bowling him over. It didn't stop, as it headed straight for Katya. Landing with a thud, Maro rolled over onto his stomach, watching the massive crocotta chase after her. She screamed and ran.

Not a bad plan.

The mother mimic leapt, and Katya slid on the ground. The beast cleared her with ease, snapping as it sailed past. Katya climbed to her feet, sprinting back to the group. Maro stood just as Katya closed the distance. A ghostly shape of darkness and orange light flickered as it came rushing forward.

"We're fucked!" Runnel yelled.

Yup.

And then, the beast landed in their midst, snapping at them. All jerked back with each movement of the head, but time and exhaustion would catch them in the end. Runnel, the slowest of the bunch, was her target of choice. She rammed him with all her weight, then climbed on top, trying to bite him.

"Get it off! Get it off!"

He jerked his head to the sides as she went for his throat. Maro sprinted over, grabbing the creature from behind, pulling with all his might.

Bitch weighs as much as an ox!

No matter how much he pulled, he only kept her from tearing out Runnel's throat. And then, Katya was there, jumping onto the beast's back, clubbing the skull with all she could muster. The crocotta's head spun, nipping at Katya, who kept hitting. In a violent movement, Katya sailed through the air, and Maro clamped down his arms around the beast's hindquarters.

He placed his legs under him, ready to strain with all his might, rearranged his arms for a better grip. A sharp pain nicked his fingers.

He winced. *Fucking bracer! Oh, stupid, stupid, stupid!*

Maro wouldn't move the beast, not with strength alone. Instead, he turned his left arm sideways, facing upward, and dragged it across the crocotta's belly with all his might. Flesh gave way, and a sickening splash of blood and guts splattered against the floor, coating Runnel from his knees down. The beast howled and tried to escape, but the palladium entered its body, and it grew weak a moment later. Its gnashing jaws stopped snapping, and it tried to crawl away.

Maro cast a quick glance at the other bounty hunter; he seemed unharmed. Stepping around the twitching beast, he pulled the gun, shoved it in the mother's ear, and pulled the trigger. Like before, the deafening roar of the single-shot pistol reverberated throughout the chamber, causing him to wince and blink back tears. He withdrew the gun from the mimic's ear canal, finding everything up to his elbow covered in blood and brain matter.

Damn the Autarch. Bitch's head was as big as my whole chest!

"You!" Runnel said from the ground, his breath ragged.

"Yeah," Maro replied, stepping back. He grimaced. "I know, I killed it. We're lucky as hell as it is."

"You!" the Mium repeated, getting to his feet and closing the distance between them. He rushed forward, wrapping Maro up in an iron-clad embrace. "You saved me!"

"Can't breathe," Maro squeaked. If he ever doubted who'd win in a fight, he was certain now. Bloodbane shook him back and forth like a rag doll. "Let go," he whispered, trying to draw air.

"Clever man! Smart for me to bring you! Good cook, good jokes, good fight!"

"You're hurting me." Bloodbane shook him all the more. "Katya's hurt!"

At her name, Runnel released him. "Where? Where's she-devil? She needs hug, too."

Maro took a few deep breaths, his ribs aching. "You might kill the poor girl."

Runnel laughed his belly-jiggling 'huh huh huh,' and wagged a finger. "I never tire of jokes."

The mimic twitched. Maro jumped, spinning around, pointing his empty gun at the smaller creature. A yelp escaped its mouth. "Damn the Autarch! I'll piss myself before this is over."

Bloodbane stood rigid too, ready to fight. "Never trust anything; creatures play dead. I'll do baby one." Runnel breathed out a sigh of relief and punched Maro on the arm. "Go to Katya."

Maro winced from the pain, but he didn't need to be told twice. *Another damn war wound. Who did more damage? The monster or Runnel?*

He left Bloodbane to deal with the sicker aspects of collecting their bounty, and hurried over to Katya.

She was rousing, holding her head as he knelt beside her. "What happened?" she asked.

"I saved your ass; you should've seen it."

She gave a single chuckle through the nose. "I doubt it. Every chance, you're always lying around."

Yeah, your invitation to climb on top of me.

"Hidden talent of mine."

"Any other talents I'm not aware of?"

Yes, I fuck up everything I touch.

Instead, he said, "You'll have to stick around to find out."

"Enticing me with mystery?"

He gave her a single, mirthful chuckle, and pulled her to her feet. "Just promising an adventure, unless this whole bounty hunting thing has turned you off to that sort of thing."

She winced as she moved her arm, massaging her shoulder with her other. "Monster hunting's not my thing."

Damn, that's a pity. It would've been nice to have her on the trail with me.

Of course, if she was, he wouldn't get much done.

"Come on," he said. "Bloodbane should be done by now."

They returned as Runnel wrapped three prismatic gems into a handkerchief, and the last of the creature melted away. Little of the mother remained, but being far larger, elements of her passing were still visible.

He stayed squatting for a moment, gazing at the closed cloth, and passed it to Maro. "For you." Confused, he opened his hand, and Bloodbane deposited it in his palm.

"Why?"

Runnel stood. "You saved me. No money can repay; this helps."

"Yeah, but—"

Runnel held up a hand to stave off the argument. "Without you, no more women. I find more money. I thought I bury you; instead, you almost bury me. Take bounty, but if tale comes up, tell everyone Bloodbane was here, too."

He smirked. "That's the least I can do."

Runnel nodded and shooed them away. "Go. You have long ride back to Tepress."

"What about you?" Katya asked. "You're not going back to Tepress?"

Bloodbane pulled on his long, curly beard and shook his head.

"No, Maro's bounty. No reason. I go Beausol."

"Damn, that's months away by wagon!"

Bloodbane dipped his head in acknowledgement.

"Yes, but many stops, more bounties and women."

Maro grinned. It didn't sound like a terrible life, hitting the trail, collecting bounties, never having to see the same woman again unless you wanted to. His eyes darted to Katya.

She glared at him.

He cleared his throat, and whatever vestiges of a smile he had melted away.

"Safe travels, Bloodbane."

He held out his hand.

"Please!" the other said, holding out his arms. "We're family now, yes? Brothers! We hug; you call me Runnel."

"Last hug cracked my ribs."

Bloodbane shrugged. "I was exciting!"

"Excited," Maro corrected.

The foreigner pulled him into another embrace, and he could've sworn he heard his back pop. When he let go, Runnel turned his arms wide to Katya, but she already had her hand proffered instead. Runnel deflated a bit, but he took the gesture.

They all returned to the entrance of the cave to find the rain had let up. The soggy ground held numerous puddles of muddy water. Clouds still rolled overhead, darkening the dawn light, but at any moment, the Autarch could turn on the faucet again.

"Maro?" Runnel said, jerking him to a halt.

"Yeah?"

"I still want saddle. Perhaps you give me?"

He cracked a smile. "Go buy your own. Mine's not for sale."

"Ah, but you have gems."

Maro shook his head. "How am I supposed to reach Tepress? Walk?"

"Good for health."

"Sorry."

Runnel narrowed his green eyes and gave a shallow nod. "Next time, you give saddle. I pay nice price."

He smiled, then slapped Maro on the arm, causing him to stagger a step.

Damn, that's going to leave another bruise.

Bloodbane lumbered off to his wagon, and Maro eyed Katya.

"You still hunting for Atine's Reservoir?"

She peered back at the cave and shook her head.

"Are you kidding? After everything we went through?"

He grunted. "Yeah, never know when there are more monsters lurking in the dark."

"I know; that's why I'm going back with you."

He cocked an eyebrow. "That's bold of you to assume. Besides, didn't you call me a monster?"

She shrugged. "That was before I knew you. Besides, you like me well enough."

Looking at you, maybe, don't know about your personality, though.

He frowned while searching for his ride. "Where's Bitch?"

Katya's brows shot up.

"You named your horse Bitch?"

"Yeah."

"Why on Atar would you name her Bitch?"

"Cause she's a mare, and the other one's already named Bastard."

Katya cracked a smile at that.

"Come on, she's this way."

"The saddle better be there when I arrive!"

Chapter 9: Man Of Few Words

Those who hoard wealth are the declared enemy of all who are without, those who give away money without thought are fools, those who take what isn't theirs are the adversary of law; guard against this totalitarian greed and deal with fanatical zeal. Cursed is the one who takes what isn't theirs—The Book of Greed, The Sacral Compendium.

Riding into Tepress—with Katya seated at his back—didn't have the same appeal Maro once associated with the town, not that the dying settlement held much to begin with. But it'd taken him in when he left the army and started over, so the place nestled in the one soft spot in his shriveled, hollow heart. Though still new to the bounty hunting business, Tepress settled over him like a moldy, dust-caked blanket, or a guest who'd long overstayed their welcome.

In Maro's brief adult life, he'd been on the move, shuffling between one forward encampment to the next, spending weeks in the bush, on the trail, making friends with shrubs and stones that'd stab him in the back while he slept. A hot meal became an anomaly, a rarity long forgotten, cherished in only faded memories like the scent of a woman you once loved.

To say Tepress flourished like a rotting corpse serviced a lie; it was far from dead … for now. But the death knell struck many years prior. All told, it'd never rise to be anything more prominent and only drag its victims into the cold obscurity of nothing. It reached its pinnacle two scores before, and it'd languish in its death throes for years to come.

It boiled down to opportunity and location.

The town sat on the edge between two well-established cusps: the ass-end of nowhere, and beyond—which amounted to rough country for countless leagues, mapped-out shit holes, and large swaths of wilderness between.

Maybe Runnel's got the right idea, head out and hit a bigger area, more cities and civilization. Not all the way to Beausol, but it's a start.

The thought of civilization didn't sit well with him. Civility evaded him from his time in the cradle, and the sins of his youth would mark him among the throngs like ink stains on a silk shirt, an affront to the hoi polloi. He doubted he could slip in and pick up a life he'd never known, but living in Tepress would take him down, too.

"It stinks," Katya said from behind him. Manure, hay, and the stench of horses clustered together in the town stable at the south end; mud and countless people mixed in a potent quagmire of nostril vomit.

Hard to smell it while living here, but a few days out in the country will clean you out. Can't miss it when coming back.

He wondered how the cities managed, and if those places smelled any better.

More people means more shit.

Katya's arms hugged him as they rode double. He glanced at the town budding to life in the early morning hours. They could've made it in last night, but the ungodly hour would ensure no proper establishments were open, so they opted for one last night on the trail. This morning's trek hadn't been but two hours, and the grey daybreak promised a slow start for all involved.

The aroma of baked bread hit him about as hard as the crocotta that jumped on his chest in the cave, and his stomach grumbled a soggy plea for him to ride over and devour the baker's rising cache. There'd been little to eat the night before, nothing but jerky, and both he and Katya went to sleep disgruntled. While they huddled in their blankets, freezing despite the fire, he thought about offering her the choice of sharing body warmth, but somehow, he didn't think that'd be the adventure she always talked about.

Well, I could've had an adventure …

But his scent probably rivaled stagnant swamp water.

He grunted in response to her declaration. She was right, of course, about the Tepress's aroma, but it didn't warrant verbal commiserating.

"You don't talk much, do you?" she asked.

He shook his head.

"I like that. Man of few words."

"It's something you should look into."

She laughed and gave him a soft smack on his back. "Makes winning an argument easier. Now, I understand what Runnel was talking about. You're pretty funny … for an asshole."

Well, she's on target.

"I ain't an asshole, just intolerant. Besides, right now, you smell like one."

She guffawed. "Rude! And you're not much better."

He nodded. "Keeps the mosquitos away."

Women, too.

Maro steered Bitch to the hitching post outside the guild. Katya slipped down, and he climbed out of the saddle, his feet landing in soggy mulch. With legs sore from the saddle, cold, and damp, and other parts in such a ghastly state, he didn't want to think about it too much.

Nice hot tub will fix me up right.

He tied the mare to the post and turned to face Katya.

"Here we are," he said.

Good one, Maro. Really witty banter to keep her engaged.

"Here we are," she echoed.

"Am I going to see you again, or are you taking off on another adventure?"

That's a little better. Don't shit the bed, you little twit.

She shrugged. "I take a little downtime in between trips. Right now, I'm going to go soak in a bath for two days to get the stench out of my hair. I'll be around while deciding what to do."

He nodded. *Shit, find some way to turn this into another meeting.*

He waved a hand, indicating the direction up the road. "How about we grab some grub at The Hormoans before you take off?"

She gave him a curious glance, as if unsure of what she'd heard. "Was that 'the hormones' or 'the whore moans?'"

He shrugged. "Take your pick. Both are apt. It's the bounty hunter's place of choice."

She cocked an eyebrow. "And which are you hoping for? Rampant hormones or—"

"It's just a name."

She smiled at his discomfort. "Will they let me in?"

"You'll be with me. No hunter worth his salt turns down the opportunity for coin."

Or a damn fine-looking woman.

Katya tipped her head toward his hat. "So, you going to give me that for services rendered?"

He smiled as a salacious thought entered his mind, but that was the problem. Usually, what he thought came out of his mouth, kind of like now.

"Sure, right after I talk you out of your clothes, then you can model it for me."

She laughed, something warm and full of mirth, her dazzling teeth bright in the early morning light. Collecting her pack from Bitch's saddle, she said, "See you around, asshole."

He dipped his head. "Katya."

He watched her go, shambling up the grimy road, walking off the saddle soreness. Either that, or someone would blame him for her gait. She cut a fine figure, and if he could find a woman like her who could withstand his profession and past, that might be a woman worth hitching his life to. Problem lay in finding one. All the ethnicities had quirks about them, his included. Not only could he face a potential culture clash, but if their Houses didn't align, and a woman couldn't stomach his demerit of intolerance, it might be a rocky trail to navigate.

"Farewell, Katya," he whispered to himself.

It'd been a bizarre few days, and he wasn't keen on repeating them, not unless Katya or some other hot mess manifested on the trail. The mimics terrified him, were vicious little bastards, and it wasn't an experience to repeat.

I ain't ever hunting those again.

Walking to the mare's front, he stroked her jaw. "I'll be a little bit, Bitch, then we'll find you some fresh hay."

Bitch dipped her head and whinnied.

"Oh, so you understand me?"

She blew out a breath.

"And that's why I named you Bitch, 'cause people would look at me funny if I called you Cunt."

Stepping up the creaking steps to the faded white door, he pushed it open to the familiar jangle of bells overhead. Horace materialized almost two breaths later.

"Maro!" he said jovially. "Ya ain't dead."

The ex-soldier nodded as he sauntered over to the counter. "Yeah, well, it ain't from lack of opportunity."

That timeless, comforting scent of the guild washed over him: leather, gun oil, and sawdust. He'd never grow tired of it. The shop remained unchanged since day one, minus the wares. They still hung the single-shot pistols on the walls, lazy L-shape designs, the longer original muskets, and some newer double-barrel guns. Knives still stuffed the glass cases near the back of the room.

Drallus entered the room. "Is that Maro, I hear?" When the guild master laid eyes on him, he beamed. "Maro, my boy! How was your adventure? Still in one piece?"

"Hmm. More or less. Damn frightening experience."

"What d'ya hunt?" Horace asked.

"Crocottas."

Both Horace and Drallus gave meaningful sounds in the back of their throats. The guild master spoke, "Vicious little bastards."

Ain't that the truth?

He reached into his coat pocket and pulled out the folded cloth holding the three prism gems and showed the two men. "Bloodbane said I could take the bounty, if one's to be had. He didn't tell me about removing the eyes before they died, so I botched it."

Drallus nodded. "One of the more disgusting aspects. Not every creature's as devious."

"Ya only got three eyes," Horace noted, pointing out the obvious.

"You can count?"

The manager shrugged. "How do we know ya got them? Ain't but three eyes."

Maro tilted his head to the side and gazed down at him.

"Think I stop halfway on the second one and think, 'Nah, I'm good?'"

"Horace?" Drallus said. "Pay the man. Maro's been straight with us since day one."

"Thanks."

Drallus nodded to the prisms. "Keep the single gem. Might be a pretty crown when you're in a rough patch."

While Horace doled out the crowns, he plucked it from the countertop and stuffed it in his pocket.

"How was it like working with Bloodbane?" Drallus asked.

"Wasn't too bad. He's quite meticulous with his wagon's orderliness."

Drallus nodded.

"The hardest part: understanding that thick accent."

Horace laid down a rune with a clink. Both guild workers eyed him.

"Pardon?" Horace said.

"His accent," Maro repeated. "Hard as hell to understand him."

"What accent?" Drallus asked.

Maro frowned. "Have you never talked to the man?"

Both of them nodded, but Horace spoke, "He doesn't have an accent."

A creeping cold traveled up Maro's spine. "What?"

Drallus shook his head. "Bloodbane doesn't have an accent. Never has. It's quite shocking for a Mium, but he might've lived somewhere more local."

"What's he look like?" Horace asked.

Maro took a deep breath and let it out through his nose. "Big guy, a bit shorter than me. Long scraggly black beard that goes to his collarbone. Same tangled mess on his head." He mimicked with his hands. "Got a gut."

"That," Drallus said in measured cadence, "sort of sounds like him. It's possible he grew out his hair and beard—definitely a dark mess. But the hair? I'm not so sure. He wears it around your length, Maro."

"When's the last time you saw him?" Maro asked them.

They both shook their heads, thinking. "At least a year ago," Horace conceded.

"That's a good chunk of time for hair to grow out."

Drallus laughed. "His hair must grow faster than grass."

Something didn't sit right with Maro, and Horace's words jarred him. "Wait! Did you say it's been a year since you've seen him?"

Horace nodded. "Yeah."

"Bloodbane said he'd heard of me. I wasn't a member but nine months ago. How'd he know about me?"

Horace shrugged. "Someone at The Hormoans?"

"It's possible," Drallus added. "You've made a bit of a reputation. A no-bullshit kind of guy. Rather stoic."

"Hmm."

It made little sense. Sure, Bloodbane could've heard about him from other hunters, but why would his name come up, even in passing?

"He said he was from Sindel," Maro said.

Drallus's head bobbed from side to side. "More or less."

"And he's the Mium ethnicity?"

"Yeah," Horace answered.

"It's got to be him."

"Probably is," Drallus agreed.

Maro nodded to himself. "Still don't make sense, though."

Horace shrugged. "Maybe he asked for any fresh blood in the area. Most don't want to work with him."

Maro grunted.

Why would he be asking for fresh blood? Why don't people want to work with him?

"Your money," Horace said, sliding the pile of crowns across the counter. Maro did a quick tally, counting the full two thousand crowns. He reached for the runes and paused.

Think, damn it, what are you not seeing? As Bloodbane said, 'What's the story's moral?'

He thought over their conversations.

"I doubt you're going after small game. You'll need help, and you'll have to hire other bounty hunters, and they won't work for so little. It's the best deal out there. I get to learn, take a little profit, and you reap all the fame and women you want."

Maro blinked a few times. Something was there in that conversation, but not the whole. What was he missing? The saloon came to mind—when he first met the Sional, Ciacus.

Pushing through the people, Maro made his way over to the table, pulled out a chair, and sat.

The Sional glanced at him, his movement sharp and quick, then his eyes went to Bloodbane.

"Don't worry," Runnel said in his thick accent, "friend for job."

"Indeed?" the Sional queried in a smooth voice. His eyebrow shot up, the incredulity on his face quite blatant.

"Hmm."

Did Ciacus know Bloodbane didn't have any friends, or was it something else? The accent Horace was telling me about?

"Maro?" Drallus called in a questioning voice.

"Hang on, I'm working on something." He withdrew the hand hovering over the crowns. Another memory flashed to the forefront of his mind.

Runnel dropped his pack at his feet and tossed a shovel with his other.

Maro's eyes tracked to the tool, remembering the conversations with Horace and Drallus. "What's the shovel for?"

Runnel's gaze went to the wooden haft, and he shrugged. "Just me, I wouldn't bring."

"So, what's it for?"

Runnel rubbed his belly. "Two reasons: we dig hole for shit, and I bury you."

But they were gone for about two days and a morning, and neither he nor Bloodbane had defecated during that time, at least that he knew of. In fact, trail food plugged everyone up.

Katya's eyes darted between the two bounty hunters. "Fair enough. I'm out here hunting for Atine's Reservoir."

Runnel laughed, slapping his knee. "So stupid."

Maro glanced between the two. "What the hell's that?"

Katya's lips thinned, but Runnel spoke. "Atine's Reservoir; a myth."

"It's not a myth," Katya retorted. "I'm close! I know I am!"

"You think," Runnel continued, "he had treasure, and hid it out here? Middle of nowhere?"

"Can you think of a better place?" she countered.

Maro blinked. *No, it can't be!*

They returned in time to see Runnel wrap three prismatic gems into a handkerchief and watch the last of the creature melt away. Little of the mother remained, but being far larger, elements of her passing were still visible.

Runnel stayed squatting for a moment, gazing at the closed cloth, then handed it to Maro. "For you."

Confused, Maro opened his hand, and Runnel deposited it in his palm.

"Why?" he'd asked.

Runnel stood. "You saved me. No money can repay, but this helps."

"Yeah, but—"

Runnel held up a hand to stave off the argument. "Without you, no more women. I find more money. I thought I'd bury you; instead, you almost buried me. Take bounty, but if tale ever comes up, tell everyone Bloodbane was here, too."

Maro smirked. "That's the least I can do."

Runnel nodded and shooed them away. "Go. You have long ride back to Tepress."

"What about you?" Katya asked. "You're not going back to Tepress?"

Bloodbane pulled on his long, curly beard and shook his head. "No, Maro's bounty. No reason. I go Beausol."

"Maro?" Horace asked.

One last detail clicked into place. Katya healed him, and when he realized they were in a cave, she'd said Bloodbane found it.

How would he know about the cave? Hell, I didn't. Katya didn't seem too surprised, but she hunted Atine's Reservoir. Unless…

93

"Holy fucking Autarch," Maro breathed. He blinked a few times, lifting his gaze to the other two. He slammed his fist down on the countertop. "Damn the Autarch!"

"What?" Horace asked.

"I know why he wanted me, asked about me. I'm new here, not only to the business, but to the area."

"Yeah, so?" Horace prodded.

"What's something rumored to be around here?"

Horace shrugged, but Drallus answered, "Atine's Reservoir."

Maro nodded.

"Yeah, right," Horace said, laughing. "Ya think he knows where it's at?"

"He brought a shovel with him," Maro said, his words coming fast. "Said he'd bury me should I die. He seem to be the generous type?"

The other two shook their heads.

"He let me have the bounty, free and clear, all two thousand crowns, and that's after he whined and bitched about me taking a twenty percent cut." Maro rubbed his eyes with one hand. How could he have been so blind?

Stupid, stupid, stupid!

Runnel's words filled his head. *"Never trust anything, creatures play dead."*

I shouldn't have trusted him. That's the damn moral of the story!

"Damn him! He shooed us out of the cave after we finished. Reminded us of the long trip back to Tepress."

"And ya think it's in these caves?" Horace's face held a reddening scowl mixed with a touch of aghast.

Why are you making that face? It ain't like Bloodbane duped you, jackass!

Maro hadn't even considered that. When he thought about caves, an image of being surrounded by rock filled his mind, but not all were solid rock. Due to rain, erosion, and water seeping through above and entrance, they had puddles and dirt within.

"Maybe," he admitted. He focused on Drallus. "How much is rumored to be in Atine's Reservoir?"

Drallus's eyebrows lifted, and he blinked several times before he answered. "Some estimates say a hundred-thousand crowns; most assume more."

Maro stopped breathing. He'd been near a fortune and never the wiser. Was that why Runnel had always been ahead of them? He didn't stay with the group, but went out on his own, scouting, risking his life to find little details.

"I've got to go," he said. In a rush, he scooped up a five-crown wick and five one-crown chits, shoving the rest back to Horace. "I'll be back for this."

"Don't do anything foolish!" Drallus yelled as Maro bolted through the door. Outside, he rode Bitch back to the stable, tossed the boy two aluminum chits—an overkill for the tasks he'd be performing—gave him instructions and hurried to the general goods store. Inside, he slapped down the three remaining wicks and barked his order to the old man standing behind the counter.

"I'll be back in fifteen minutes. I've got to go, so have it ready!" He ran out the door.

At home, he threw his pack on his bed, upended it, and dumped the contents over his wool blanket. Stripping out of his reeking, damp clothes, he kicked his legs out, waddling like a duck to free his legs from the trousers. Naked, he hurried to dress again, and after, stuffed his pack with more clothes.

Dashing back to the store, he scooped up his order of jerky, a block of cheese, a jar of peanut butter, and a sack of pecans into the top of his bag. Back at the stables, he found Bastard saddled and ready for him. The old horse fidgeted with anticipation.

"You ready, Bastard?" Maro asked as he tied the pack to the saddle.

Bastard snorted.

"We gotta ride hard, old timer. You up for it?"

Bastard bobbed his head, nuzzled Maro for an affection pat, and held still as he climbed into the saddle.

"Yeah, I missed you, too. Bitch doesn't have a personality; that's why you're the better horse."

Boot heels kicked into his steed's flanks and they were gone, riding back to the caves he'd left the day before.

Maro and Bastard made damn good time, arriving an hour after night fell in earnest. Both were worn out, but Bastard seemed to grow stronger as the journey progressed. Perhaps it was the prolonged reprieve, or that his body remembered all those years on the trail.

He's got more fat stores since he's been sitting in the stable most of the time.

Ensuring his musket-pistol was loaded, and the knife still hung at his belt, Maro addressed his horse. "Don't do anything stupid while I'm gone."

Bastard shook his mane.

"I mean it!" Maro said, pointing at the ground. "You better be here when I return."

Bastard stared at him.

"No funny business, or I'll make jerky out of you."

Bastard looked away, his ear twitching.

With that, Maro dipped into the cave. He waded about a dozen steps in and stopped.

Damn, I can't see shit in here.

He returned to Bastard, who still stared at the cave's mouth like he expected Maro to return.

"I don't want to hear it," Maro said as he reached for the pack.

Bastard gave a sharp, short whinny.

"Hey, I said I don't want to hear it." Reaching inside the bag, Maro pulled his flint and steel, struck them together, and the shower of sparks turned into a flame. He glanced at the horse as he stuffed the flint and steel into his left coat pocket. He noted the horse's ears were flat back. "What?"

Bastard looked away.

"I ain't going to turn you to jerky out here. Only when we get back, and that's if you don't behave!" Fire in the palm of his left hand, gun drawn in his right, Maro reentered the cave.

It didn't take him long to retrace the path where they killed both mimics, and once there, he spied footprints leading deeper into the cave, past the small chamber where the final battle took place. Maro hurried forward, holding the flames high. He came to a branch which forked in many directions, at least half a dozen, and each path displayed footprints save one.

He took another step forward, and his foot sunk a hair's breadth. He stepped back, peering down.

What the hell? Sand? A lot of it.

It looked like the water-laden sand at the beach, beaten down by the repetition of the tide. He peered up at the branching tunnels.

"I guess we're going to be difficult …"

He hurried down the first one on the left. Much to his delight and dismay, the second path he traversed revealed evidence of Bloodbane's prolonged occupation. Leaning against the wall stood his shovel, and in the floor, a massive hole had been dug out, earth and stone removed and piled high.

"Fucked twice on the holy day…"

Maro gazed down into the hole, every murderous thought flowing through him.

Son of a bitch deceived me!

Maro paused, asking himself if he would've told Katya of the cache's location had it been his. Would he tell Katya now, to give her the satisfaction of knowing she'd been right? Or would that rend her heart all the more, knowing it lay within her grasp?

Bloodbane's voice floated in the back of his mind. *"Never trust anything; creatures play dead."*

Maro nodded to himself. *Yeah, that's the moral of the story, don't trust anyone. I bought Runnel's story, hook, line, and sinker.*

He should've known it didn't tally right.

He used me to kill the guardians of the treasure and hurried me off so he could dig it up alone. What a bastard!

Every tale held a moral, whether people admitted it or not. Moving forward, it'd be the center most thought to keep in mind.

So, what am I going to do? What's going to be the moral of the story?

He could end it here and now, walk away, leave the tale unresolved. He'd still be alive, wounded by his own naivety and stupidity, a blow to his pride, or he could chase Runnel to the ends of Atar to collect his due. But what claim did Maro have to Atine's Reservoir? Did he have any more right to it than Runnel or Katya?

No, it wasn't about a right or claim. That came secondary and paled next to the genuine issue. Maro couldn't abide this slight. His demerit of intolerance wouldn't let him, pride be damned! A wrong had to be righted.

That's one dead son of a bitch when I find him.

Exiting the cave, he mounted up and scanned the darkness for the wagon trail.

"Come on, Bastard, we ain't done by half, and you're gonna hate my ass before we're through!"

Chapter 10: Retribution

Retribution is not the same as vengeance, for one is a justice served for a wrong, and the other is an act of passion laced with greed and malice. Transgress not when seeking requital—The Book of Retribution, The Sacral Compendium.

Maro stepped up to the snoring figure, knelt beside him, and stuck the pistol barrel in his snoring mouth.

Bloodbane came awake, his face slack as he gagged around the musket's business-end, and the dim firelight brought out the darkness in his wide eyes.

"Morning, sunshine," Maro grumbled.

By the gods, he was tired. His body ached with fatigue, his knees were sore from the stirrups, his back ached with a permanent hunch, and a grubby fog settled over his mind. So completely spent—wanted nothing more than to find a soft rock to curl up on, or even return to the hovel he called home. But no, unfinished business awaited. Two days without sleep will drive any man to the breaking point or into the arms of madness, and right now, he wanted Bloodbane to see him teetering on the edge of lawlessness.

And none of this accounted for Bastard's orneriness. That little shit made the last few hours miserable; irritation stemmed from age and weariness. Maro hovered on the verge of shooting the poor beast in the ass to keep him moving. He'd make it up to his mount some way, or he could kiss their partnership goodbye.

Bastard holds grudges.

"Now," Maro said, talking in low tones, "imagine my surprise when I get back to the guild house and learn you don't have an accent. None of them can recall one. Oh, yeah, and you screwed me out of the biggest find in centuries."

Runnel tried to say something around the barrel, but Maro tsked him into silence.

"You know, I don't begrudge your find. My compliments. But what really chaps my ass is the way you mocked Katya, pretending the treasure didn't exist, all while hunting it yourself. Hell, you had a good notion, and that's why you let me tag along."

Maro rolled his head in a circle, feeling his neck crackle under the movement as the waves of drowsiness crashed against him.

"You made me doubt her intelligence, second guess my judgement, mocked my trust, and took advantage of my ignorance. That's something I just can't abide—something I can't tolerate."

Runnel shook his head fractionally, mumbling a plea for mercy.

"If you would've told me what you're after, I might've laughed or scoffed, but I wouldn't have tried to take it from you. I have morals. I might've insisted on taking the bounty for the crocottas, which you gave me in the end—nice touch by the way, getting me to leave without making a scene, without questioning—maybe even pushed to take a piece of fabled treasure, but I would've never stooped so low to steal from you. And had Katya not been there, you would've killed me to keep your secret."

He paused, letting out a weary sigh.

"Greed enables men to become monsters to each other, and it makes fools of us all."

Maro swallowed as he lifted his head, scanning the night for predators or friends of Runnel, but he didn't count on the latter. Perhaps Ciacus, but he doubted that. If this whole episode was anything to judge by, whatever friends Runnel had were ancient history. He gazed down at the pale Mium.

"But the real reason you wanted us away? Because Katya hunted the treasure, and you don't share. What'd you say? You have a certain 'lifestyle?' She would've taken half of your kingdom, but half a kingdom's better than none. You screwed her, and not the 'hey, let's have a poke' kind of way."

Maro's eyes narrowed as he gazed into Runnel's frigid emerald eyes. They were dark with fury. Maro's right thumb cocked the hammer, the moving metal parts sounding loud in the muted gloom. The crickets hushed long enough to let it reverberate, and the snap-hiss of the fire seemed to applaud the move. Runnel's eyes shifted from anger to terrified.

"I've done a lot of things I ain't proud of—can't begin to count how many men I've put in the ground. I've tortured them, cut off fingers, left them bleeding out, burned the face off one jackass named Wesley, and took from them after they stopped breathing. Never once did I have qualms about doing so. It was upright from my view, for a greater cause, and I swore off the path. But this?" He shook his head. "Well, this is just personal."

Maro tensed his shoulders, leaning into the gun. Runnel mumbled something louder, groveling for a chance to speak.

Maro shifted his body away, leaning back. "I could've been your friend, Bloodbane. Guess we'll never find out."

He straightened his arm, tilted his head away from the impending splash of blood. Runnel held up his hands, holding them together in one final desperate attempt.

He sighed and rolled his eyes. "You're probably about to say everything I've ever heard before, so you better make this count. Open wide."

Bloodbane did, and Maro extracted the pistol from his mouth.

"Take it," Runnel said in his authentic voice. "All of it."

"Well, look at that. You *don't* have an accent. And you can speak in complete sentences. Was Ciacus in on the plan?"

"No. I've always used an accent with him, too."

Well, at least there's one less person I've got to chase down.

Maro shook his head.

"Take all the treasure? And what? Leave you alive, pissed off, and aiming for my back? Not a chance. Dead's the only sure way."

"Fine! Don't take all of it! Take what you want and leave me the rest."

"And what's to keep you from coming after me once I do?"

Runnel was silent for a moment. When he spoke, the bitterness of his words couldn't be missed.

"If I were to lay hands on you, I'd crush the life out of you, but you're too sharp, and you'd kill me long before I reach you."

Maro let his eyes drift up to the rolling clouds. Stars sparkled between the dark cotton swirls.

He nodded, returning his gaze to Bloodbane.

"Ain't that the truth? Tell you what. I'll take what I deem fair for making an ass out of me. And when next we meet, I won't give you the benefit of the doubt."

He leaned in close.

"I'll gun you down, 'cause I can never trust you again, and you burned all second chances with me. If I don't put a bullet in your head the moment I lay eyes on you, I'll cut off your balls and shove them down your fucking throat for the aggravation you caused me."

Bloodbane nodded.

"Now," he said, making a shooing motion with his pistol, "you lay back down, 'nice and easy' like you like. That chest in the wagon, the reservoir?"

Runnel did as told.

"Yes."

Maro peeled back Runnel's blanket, snatching up the man's pistol. He stood and chucked it into the woods.

"So, you don't have any gallant ideas once I ride out."

"Rifle's in the wagon."

Maro nodded.

"Not anymore. I dealt with that one before I woke you up."

He backed away until he reached the wagon. Keeping his right arm aimed in his general direction, he called a flame from the campfire to his awaiting hand. With fire in his left palm, he holstered the pistol. If Bloodbane tried anything, he'd be seared alive.

Latch flicked, he pulled the lid open. The insides of the chest glittered. Gold, silver, diamonds, sapphires, rubies, emeralds, amethysts, pearls, necklaces, bracelets, amulets, all shined brightly in the orange light.

"Hmm."

A small fortune, far beyond anything he or Drallus suspected. A handful would make Maro richer than he'd ever been, wealthier than ever dreamed. But it wasn't about him. He wasn't seeking for his own benefit. It boiled down to righting a wrong.

No price can set that right.

Within all the glittering, two items twinkled in his eyes.

I hope a curse follows this bastard wherever he goes.

Maro glanced up from the chest, spotting Runnel still lying there. He shook his head.

"Bloodbane, you're going to drink and whore yourself to death."

Runnel responded in his accent, echoing the words the first night they met.

"I have lifestyle."

Maro harrumphed. "Yeah, for as short as it'd last." He shook his head again. "If I were you, I'd bury this. You go toting it around ... not everyone's going to be noble."

He reached inside and plucked the two items he'd been eyeing. Once snug in his coat pocket, he closed the lid.

"Next time I see you, Runnel, I'm going to assume you're there to kill me; don't be upset when I put you down first."

Runnel sat up on his bedroll and dropped his fake accent.

"All considered, it could've been a lot worse. I'll consider us even."

Yeah, no shit. I give you your life and you keep all the treasure.

"That's nice."

Maro whistled, and Bastard came trotting up from the darkness. Bastard eyed the flame in Maro's hand. He extinguished the fire, pulled his pistol, aiming for Bloodbane, and climbed up into the saddle.

"And no, it still ain't for sale."

Runnel laughed, his deep, belly jiggling 'huh huh huh.' "I can afford any price."

"Some things ain't for sale, no matter the price."

"Take care, Maro."

Yeah, I'll be watching my back from here on out.

With a dip of his head, he kicked Bastard's flanks and disappeared into the night.

Epilogue

Find joy in each other's company, for I have made you as two halves to a whole. Condemn the one who seeks strife where none need be found—The Book of Obedience, The Sacral Compendium.

Maro had just returned home from his bath when a knock intruded upon his solitude. His eyes went to the sound, then the bedpost, spotting his holstered pistol. Slipping it free, he held it in his right hand, and with light steps, went to the door. He cracked it open a sliver, peering through to see who was on the other side.

Katya stood with a bemused expression. When Maro didn't open the door wider, her brows rose. "Aren't you going to invite me inside?"

"Hmm." He motioned her inside, and she slipped through as he shut and bolted it behind her.

"Paranoid much, or you trying to keep me from escaping?" she teased.

When he faced her, the humor left her face, and her eyes darted down, noting the gun in his hand.

"By the Autarch, Maro, you seem more at ease on the trail."

"Want a confession? I might've made an enemy recently."

She nodded, her gaze falling to the floor.

"When a girl doesn't commit to plans, or drops hints about being in town only for a little while, that's your cue to pursue."

He grunted.

"Ain't got time for childish games. If a woman wants to be with me, she will be. If she toys with me, expects a mind reader, she ain't worth my time or trouble. That shit's just aggravating."

"Not everyone's as forward as you."

He shrugged.

"Or as cut and dry."

He stared at her for a heartbeat longer than comfortable. She opened her mouth to speak, but Maro cut her off.

"Listen, I uh—had to take care of some business. That's why I didn't come around."

She nodded.

"I saw you ride out of here like the Cursed were chasing you."

He frowned.

"Well, when it was clear you didn't take my hints, I came to the guild house to drag you to the saloon and treat me to dinner. Depending on how that went, I thought about modeling your hat."

This drew a grin from him.

"Wouldn't that be a sight?"

She cocked an eyebrow.

"I said, depending on how dinner went."

"I got something better."

He glanced around his room, searching for his coat. Spied on the dresser, he crossed over, stuffed his hand in the right, side pocket, and grasped the two objects. He hesitated a moment, relinquished the smaller object, pulling out the larger. He crossed back over and proffered it.

"For you."

She gasped. In his hand lay a silver necklace with a circular pendant. In the center sat a ruby the size of his thumbnail encircled by diamonds. At the top and bottom, as on the left and right sides, blue sapphires half the size of the ruby completed the ensemble.

"Oh, Maro, this is far better than dinner or a hat."

He smirked.

"You ain't lying."

She glanced up into his eyes.

"Can I—touch it?"

Well, that's the plan.

He nodded and let it slip from his fingers. She held it in her palm; her face a myriad of emotions.

After a moment, he offered, "Here, let me put it on you."

She stepped to the mirror, and he came up behind her, clasping the necklace in place.

"Maro, it's incredible."

"Yeah, well, it's yours."

Her eyes widened, and she spun around to face him.

"Mine? I thought you were joking! Why?"

He shrugged.

"I fell in love with the way your neck looked when you healed me. Thought it might look charming around it."

Katya laughed.

"I doubt you fell in love with my neck."

"Guilty."

She spun back around, admiring the jewelry in the mirror.

She'll be preening for a while.

He stepped back to give her space, and she followed his movements with her eyes. Touching the necklace with her fingers, she faced him once more. Her gaze swept around his hovel, noting all the stains, rips, and weathering he'd grown accustomed to.

"Delightful place you have."

"Without a woman, no need for anything fancy."

"Well," she started, edging closer to him, "I'd say you do now, and we've got to find a nicer place than this ..." she glanced around the room again, "... shit hole."

He laughed.

Woman after my heart.

"I didn't give you that necklace so you'd drop your pants."

"No? Well, it worked wonders."

Well, you have a fortune hanging around your neck.

"Maybe I'll model this instead," she said. "Where'd you get it?"

"A story for another time."

She took another step closer and kissed him. Her breath was hot, her lips soft, and she tasted like strawberries.

"You sure you wanna do this?" he asked.

She pulled back a hair, gazing up into his eyes, and gave a small shrug.

"It'll be an adventure."

About The Author

Kyle Belote is a prior active-duty Marine, writer, musician, and painter. He's lived in Texas, Hawaii, and Okinawa, Japan, and has traveled the globe. When not writing, he enjoys sketching, researching companies and investing, and reading and listening to audiobooks. Kyle enjoys a diverse collection of films, books, and shows—just not the abomination called Disney Star Wars.

For more information, please visit: www.outpostdire.com

Back Jacket Blurb

"You know, I've done a lot of things I ain't proud of—can't begin to count how many men I've put in the ground—and I never had any qualms about doing so. But this? Well, this is just personal."

Nine months after walking away from war and the gutted remains of the Lanton gang, Maro Prakk's ready to sink his teeth into something nasty—something that bites back.

On the edge of the known map, he takes a job that pays more, but survival isn't guaranteed.

Creatures stalk the wilds—something ancient, fast, and hungry. And no matter how much ammo you carry, some things don't stay dead and buried.

Bloodbane is the second brutal entry in the Maro Prakk saga.

www.ingramcontent.com/pod-product-compliance
Lightning Source LLC
Chambersburg PA
CBHW022039170626
46808CB00003B/1275